# Lost And Found

A DEEPLY EMOTIONAL AND HEARTBREAKING STORY, A JOURNEY TO FINDING LOVE AFTER LOSS, FRIENDS TO LOVERS, SINGLE DAD ROMANCE. (FINDING FOREVER SERIES BOOK 1)

## C.SMITH

C. Smith
x

# Contents

# Trigger Warnings

Lost and Found features some difficult topics, such as; discussions on grief, infertility (no losses, procedures or treatment detailed on page), violent situations including; drugging, attempted sexual assault, holding a person captive (not overly detailed on page).

For bereavement support, please contact Mind.

For support for survivors of sexual assault, please contact The Survivors Trust.

For support on coping with infertility, please contact National Infertility Support & Information Group.

## **<u>Foreword</u>**

**Due to adult content, this novel is recommended for readers 18+.**

Dedication

*For anybody who is feeling a little lost, hang in there. Someday you'll find somebody or something that makes you feel found.*

# Prologue

## Sophie

Have you ever been so lonely that it's bone deep? So over-whelming that you cannot take a breath without the physical pain overwhelming your body. That's me, that's my everyday life, feeling like I'm trapped in a bottomless pit of despair.

In general I have always considered myself a happy person, content with life. I never felt the need to surround myself with lots of friends. I grew up as an only child, I've always been used to being alone and I have grown to be comfortable in my own company.

I've been with Liam for the better part of my life, spending the last ten years living the life of a doting housewife and failing miserably at trying to become a mother.

Liam and I met in high school, we had been around each other for the majority of our childhoods but I remember really taking notice of him during our final year of school. He changed from being a boy to a man. Tall, dirty blond hair, a little scruff on his chin and he had definitely started to bulk out, he wasn't the tall scrawny kid any more. He turned into a beautiful man.

I guess he had felt the same way about me, I'd grown from a little girl and turned into a woman. Didn't help that I was a late bloomer. My boobs didn't come in until I was sixteen but when they did, let's just say the wait was worth it. That's when the boys started noticing me and Liam was at the front of that queue.

That's when life was much more simple, nowadays the heart-break of dealing with yet another negative pregnancy test every month is driving me to distraction. That's the only wish I have for my life, to become a mother. You can take the house, the cars, the holidays, the money and fancy clothes. If I could exchange it all for the chance to have a baby of my own, I'd do it in a heartbeat.

Despite my deep longing for a child, we live a reasonably happy life. We have a beautiful home, a gorgeous four bedroom house on the south coast of England with beautiful gardens which feature so many lovely rainbow coloured flowers, apple trees, a vegetable patch, swimming pool, all overlooking the ocean.

Liam works incredibly hard as a lawyer, even has his own prac-tice. I'm so incredibly proud of him and all he's achieved in order to give us a good life. He showers me with shopping sprees, gifts, holidays with my girlfriends (because obviously he's far too busy to come with me).

He works such long hours I barely see him. Usually, I'm asleep by the time he comes home and he's gone again by the time I wake. The constant negative pregnancy tests don't sound so unbelievable now huh?

Who am I to complain though, we have a beautiful life. I spend my days in the garden tending to my plants or lounging by the pool and writing my novels which I'll never have the confidence to publish. Sounds like I'm living the dream doesn't it.

So why does it all feel so wrong?

And why do I get the overwhelming feeling that shit is about to hit the fan!?

# Chapter One

**Sophie**

'Buzz Buzz, Buzz Buzz, Buzz Buzz'

Seriously, If I am woken up one more time by Liam's phone ringing off the hook in the middle of the night, I'm going to seriously lose my shit!

"Liiaaamm your phone," I moan into the darkness of our bedroom. I'm met with silence. It's usually someone from work calling with an emergency which obviously cannot wait until the morning. I mean, who thinks it's ok to call somebody in the middle of the night. Lunatics that's who! The rest of us are trying to sleep.

"Liam, will you answer your phone?". Still nothing, I slowly crack open my eyes with a deep groan and begin to sit up. When I look over to Liam's side of the bed it's empty. I slide my hand across the mattress, it feels cold. He hasn't even been to bed and looking over at my phone I notice it's two o'clock in the morning.

I hear the distant noise of the shower running in the bathroom, why on earth is he showering at two o'clock in the morning? I mean that's not entirely normal, is it? I am totally distracted by my inner monologue that I completely forgot that Liam's phone had been ringing. I'm just about to turn over and go back to sleep when the phone vibrates again with a text message. Hmm I better check it, it could be his mother, what if she's had another fall.

I lean over the bed and snatch up his phone, look down at the screen and freeze. No that can't be right, I'm not seeing what I'm actually seeing right? The text reads ...

'Baby, you left your briefcase here. Thought I'd let you know so you can swing by on your way back to the office. Maybe you can make me scream your name again if you can get out early enough? ;) T xoxo'

My whole world froze, I could feel my heart pumping so hard it's legit trying to beat out of my chest. No no no, I must be having one of my nightmares again. I have them quite often, married ladies you know the one. The one where you are locked in your own mind for hours and hours, reliving the torture of discovering that your husband is having an affair. With a younger, hotter, happier, slimmer woman who is not you! You wake up with crippling fear and paranoia swirling around your mind. Trying to convince yourself that it wasn't real, your husband wouldn't do that to you. Of course he wouldn't. Who would spend fifteen years with someone, marrying them after five, falling in love when we were teenage sweethearts, building an entire life together, trying for a family, to completely tear it down for selfish reasons like getting your dick wet!

The buzzing in my ears is getting louder, my hands are clammy, the room is starting to spin and my vision is going dark around the edges. I can feel the tension wreaking havoc on my body and the panic attack that is slamming into me with full force.

I need to get out of this room right now. I throw Liam's phone down on the bed and swing my legs over the side, I feel like my lungs are about to give out. I push to my feet but before I take another step, the phone buzzes again with another text. Don't look, don't look, just don't look I say to myself. Before I even realise what's happening, my hands are picking up the phone and there it is, the last straw that is breaking my entire heart into a million pieces. The agony ripples through my entire body as I collapse to the ground, I hear a blood curdling scream. Who was that? It was me, my entire heart has just been ripped from my body and is lying in bloody tatters on the floor.

Right there on the phone, is a photo. Not just any old photo, nope, a photo of a beautiful woman (who is not me, his wife!) dressed in gorgeous red lacy lingerie, looking into the camera with hearts in her eyes. That's bad enough right? Wrong! The worst part of the photo is when you look down and notice the blossoming baby bump taking front and centre stage.

Not only has my husband been having an affair behind my back, explains all the late nights right, but he's gotten her pregnant. He's having a baby with a woman who is not me.

And just like that, in the space of five minutes, I've learnt that my entire marriage is a lie. The betrayal is deep, so deep it feels like it's burrowing into my skin and making me question the last fifteen years of my life. I can't even move, can't bring myself to stand. It's as if my entire body is sinking into quicksand. I'll just wait here for death to take me.

# Chapter Two

**Sophie**

I hear more than see Liam come stumbling out of the bathroom in a blind panic, towel wrapped around his waist, water dripping down his chest and his hair pointing in every direction, "Baby, what's happened?" as he falls to his knees in front of me on the carpet.

I can't even bring myself to look at him, my body feels as if it's shutting down on me and all I can do is wait for it to all be over. I can't even begin to comprehend what's going on. Is this my fault? Did I cause him to cheat on me? Because I didn't give him a child.

"Sophie, talk to me baby, tell me what's wrong,". Liam is pleading with me now. I feel his warm hands cup my face and it's as if a rubber band has snapped inside me and I've gone from crippling numbness to white hot rage within a second.

"Take your lying, cheating, filthy fucking hands off of me," the snarl that leaves my mouth is dark and I barely recognise my own voice. Liam's hands drop from my face, as I raise my eyes to look into his cheating ones it's as if I'm watching it all play out on a movie screen. His eyes leave mine, flick to his open phone lying next to me on the carpet and he pieces together everything within a second. He has the absolute audacity to look hurt!

"Baby, it's not what it looks like..."

I stand to my feet, he stumbles up after me still reaching for me as if he can stop this complete shit show from happening, as if he can physically hold me together. Too late, I'm in a million pieces all over the floor.

"So, you haven't been fucking some whore behind my back? All whilst being married to me? You haven't watched my heart break every single month for years on end while we fail time and time again to have a baby? You haven't held me in your fucking arms, telling me that it'll happen when the time is right? And all the while, you're having a baby with someone else. A baby that is supposed to be growing inside of me is now growing inside of her!" I point to the offending photo still glaring at me from the carpet. My teeth are bared, my face feels hot, my body trembling as I desperately try to hold it together.

"I didn't mean for it to happen, it was an accident". Liam wipes his hand across his brow and buries his face into his hands. I can't help the disbelieving laugh that leaves my lips,

"You accidentally dropped your trousers and stuck your dick into another woman?" *Is he seriously kidding me?*

"That's not what happened. Sophie, you know me baby. We've been together for fifteen years. You know I'd never do anything to purposely hurt you". Liam takes a step forward and reaches for me. Just the thought of having his dirty hands on me sends a shiver down my spine, and not the good kind.

"How long has this been going on? And don't you dare fucking lie to me Liam. That photo is proof enough that you didn't accidentally 'fall' into her once!".

"Ten months," he says it barely above a whisper, I strain to hear him.

Oh god, this is just getting worse and worse. I think back to ten months ago, it was just before Christmas. I noticed that Liam was spending more and more time at the office. When I asked him about it he told me that he had a few new big clients that were taking up a lot of his time.

Like the doting little house wife I was, I took his word for it. Never even stopping to consider that he wasn't telling me the truth. *What a damn idiot!*

"How far along is she?".

"Seven and a half months, she's due the end of October". The breath whooshes from my lungs.

"Who is she?" I demand.

"A client, she was going through a divorce and she needed my services," he tells me.

"And she damn well got more services that she paid for by the looks of things," I shout in his face, I'm losing it. I need to reign this in a little bit, I feel like I'm going to explode. I turn away from him and walk across the room, taking a deep breath. I can hear my Mum's voice in my head, *take a deep breath baby, count to ten.* She would always say that to me as a child. I was prone to anxiety and panic attacks, being around other humans didn't sit well with me. I never felt comfortable in my own skin, never felt like I fit in anywhere, as if I could feel the nerves crawling out of my skin like a thousand tiny spiders.

Something feels like its starting to seep into my brain, a calmness beginning to spread throughout my entire body. *Thanks Mum.* She could always bring me back around, she gave me her calm and her strength. God I missed her.

Liam and I had an ok marriage, fairly boring if I'm being totally honest with myself. Now don't get me wrong, I've always loved my husband, he's all I've ever known and the only lover I've ever had. When we began to get close in high school we were inseparable and would do everything together. Not only did we fall in love, he was also my best friend.

I'd never experienced that overwhelming lust that you read about in all those romance novels, you know, where just a simple touch would send a sizzle of electricity down your spine. No, it wasn't like that for me and Liam. He was safe, he made me feel secure. He had big dreams and aspirations, *even though he never encouraged me to follow mine*, he was hard-working and I always knew that he loved me even if the chemistry between us was always a bit ... flat. Our sex life lacked passion, we had never been the type of couple to tear each others clothes off because we just had to get to each other. No it had never been like that but he was a good man, or so I thought.

Recently, that lack of chemistry had become more potent, the lack of intimacy has been killing me little by little. We lived like room-mates, not even friends, just two people who happen to live in the same house. Like two passing ships in the night.

And now I knew why.

# Chapter Three

## Sophie

My body moved on auto pilot as I strode towards my closet and grabbed two massive suitcases, heaving them onto the bed and flinging them open. Liam stood watching me, not saying a word. Fifteen years together and he couldn't even be bothered to fight for me, he must have truly given up on us.

I pressed my palm to my chest, closed my eyes and took a breath. Wow, my heart was hurting. Am I really such a terrible, unlovable person that I deserved this kind of betrayal. I just couldn't fathom where it'd all gone wrong.

I moved back to the closet, gathering my belongings, the silence beating down on me making my lungs feel tight in my chest,

"You don't have to leave, stay here, I'll leave,". Liam spoke quietly, as if walking on eggshells waiting for the rage monster to burst out of me. It wasn't there, my entire soul was destroyed. I felt numb, moving like a ghost while slowly packing more and more of my belongings.

"Already eager to set up house with your new woman?" the words should have sounded angry but I'd never felt so weak and broken, they came out quiet and flat.

"No, no...that's not what I meant Soph. I just meant that I'm the one in the wrong, I should be the one to leave".

"I want nothing from you, nothing at all except answers". I looked over to my husband. The husband I'd loved for a long time.

"Ask me anything, I'll tell you the truth".

I'm not sure why I even wanted the answers, I knew it was going to hurt. It was going to break me beyond repair. I was torturing myself by even asking.

I looked to him with tears in my eyes, my heart beating out of my chest, "Why?" I took a breath "Do you hate me that much that you wanted to completely destroy me? Did you ever love me?".

"Oh Soph". He started towards me with his arms held out, as if I'd ever be able to feel comfort in those arms ever again. I backed away, "Just answer me Liam, please".

"Of course I loved you, I still love you, you're my wife. Oh Soph, I don't even know what to say. This wasn't supposed to happen, you've just been so sad for such a long time. I know that trying for a baby has completely broken your spirit. I just don't know how to be around you anymore; feeling like I've let you down by not giving you the one thing you want more than anything. We hardly ever have sex anymore and when we do it's according to the calendar. There's no excitement between us, no passion. It just happened, Tara just came into my life and she is so full of light and happiness. It just happened and then I just couldn't stop it. I was going to tell you soon, I just didn't want to hurt you".

"Don't tell me about her, don't talk to me about how she fulfilled something in you that was missing. I don't want to know her name, I don't want to know a thing about her. She is a home wrecker nothing more. She's stolen my husband and taken everything from me". Tears were streaming down my face now. The heartbreak was tearing me in two. "I know I've been sad, but I just needed you Liam. Yes, I wanted your child more than anything in the world and I couldn't have that but I didn't have you either! You worked around the clock, came home late, we never speak, you never show an interest in me and what I was doing. You never wanted to touch me intimately. It was a transaction because you felt you had to. You never showed any interest in my writing, you sent me away on holidays. Is that when she was here? You had her here in my home, in my bed?".

"Yes," he murmured. No further explanation. I was done. I was thirty two years old, husbandless, homeless, childless, jobless. What the hell am I going to do, my minds a mess.

I didn't need anything else, there was no point in asking any further questions, it'd only break me more.

I went back to packing, all of my belongings were thrown into my bags. Lastly, I placed my seven manuscripts on the top. My prized possessions, the only thing that I'd managed to do for myself that gave me any sort of joy. Liam looked at them like he didn't even know what they were, of course he didn't. he knew nothing about me.

I didn't even bother getting dressed. I put my dressing gown on over top my pyjamas, pulled my rings off my wedding finger and pressed them into Liam's hand.

"I want a divorce, I don't want to hear from you, I don't want to see you, I want nothing from you. You set out to break me. Congratulations Liam, I'm broken". I grabbed my bags and walked out into the night.

*What the hell am I going to do now?*

## Hugh

What an absolute shit show the last two years has been. Just when life seemed absolutely perfect it was torn away cruelly and within the space of months. My wife Grace was the absolute love of my life, we met in college and the very first time I laid my eyes on her I knew that she was my forever.

We had so much fun together, spending every free moment together, going on dates, eating out, going to parties on the weekends. Our absolute favourite times were the simple, quiet moments. Lying together on a Sunday morning, talking for hours as the sun rose.

I'll never forget the day I asked Grace to marry me, it wasn't some huge elaborate proposal that you see in the movies. We lay quietly in each others arms, moments after making love to each other and the words just tumbled out "Fancy spending forever like this?". She didn't even have to answer, just snuggled closer and kissed my chest right above my heart. We were married a year later in a beautiful ceremony in the middle of a beautiful meadow filled with wild flowers. The birds and bees joined our closest family and friends, watching us make our vows, ready to spend the rest of our lives together.

That was the best day of my whole life, closely followed 5 years later when Grace told me she was pregnant, the love and excitement in her eyes when she told me. Man, I'll never forget the look on her face. We had waited until we'd both finished college and were settled in our new adult lives. We had been trying for a while to expand our family. I saw the sadness in Grace's eyes when it didn't happen straight away but we persevered and it was damn fun trying!

Nine months after that, our beautiful Lucie May was born and wow, if I thought I'd known love before that day then I was truly blown out of the water when I looked into that little girls gorgeous big brown eyes, just like her mothers. Watching her change and grow was an absolute pleasure and doing it all with Grace by my side was like a dream come true. How lucky was I.

Life was pretty amazing for the next year or so after that until Grace started to feel tired and unwell, suffering from terrible migraines and nausea. It was horrible seeing her struggle so terribly, all whilst trying to care for Lucie. I was working everyday at the station, it was my job to support us so that Grace could stay at home and raise Lucie. Old fashioned I know but that's what she wanted. She didn't want to miss a single second and I loved her all the more for it.

At first we put Grace's illness down to the exhaustion of having a small child. Lucie was pretty damn exhausting, she had just started walking and was into absolutely everything. But after a few weeks we decided to get Grace checked out at the doctors. Very quickly after that Grace was diagnosed with stage four neuroblastoma and our entire world came crashing down. Every plan for our future was gone, our entire world thrown into turmoil. I felt like I couldn't take a breath, I couldn't even begin to imagine what Grace was feeling. We held each other whilst we sobbed and hoped for a miracle. All the while knowing that it was too late for a miracle, Grace's cancer had spread into her lymph nodes, her bones and her other organs. How didn't we see it? Grace had only started to feel unwell recently and now I was going to lose my sweetheart and Lucie was going to grow up never knowing her mother.

I couldn't even begin to put into words how the next three months went. We tried various treatments to try to prolong Grace's life and make her more comfortable. All the while, trying to ensure she had the very best memories of Lucie to take with her when she left us. Grace spent her better days writing in her diary, making sure she got everything down that she wanted to leave behind. She wrote letters to Lucie for when she was older and I was under strict instruction to never let Lucie forget about her mum. As if I ever could.

By the end, Grace had come to terms with her diagnosis and found a peace in knowing that her pain would soon be over. She was so much stronger than I was. All I could see was everything that I was losing, my wife, the love of my life, my soulmate, the mother of my child.

In the last two weeks of Grace's life, she got weaker and weaker, spending more time asleep than awake. She had live in carers who would help me take care of her. I had my hands full with a fifteen month old little girl, I needed all the help I could get.

We spent our last days together snuggled on Grace's hospital bed at home, looking through hundreds of photos of our lives together. Reliving memories that we thought we were going to have our whole lives to relive over and over again. I truly believe Grace knew when her time was coming, I remember so clearly the morning before she passed. We were cuddled together, Lucie asleep on my chest, our hands clasped together around her. Grace didn't have much energy at all in the end, but she looked into my eyes and asked me to make her a promise. She asked me to find love again one day, she didn't want me to grow old alone and sad. She didn't want Lucie to grow up without a mother. My first reaction to hearing that was anger and extreme sadness. How could I ever love anybody ever again? Grace was my only love, I didn't have space in my heart for another woman. However, I saw the pleading in Grace's eyes, the strength it had taken for her to ask me. So I told my wife the only lie I'd ever told her. I promised her that one day I'd find someone to love me and Lucie, we wouldn't be alone and she didn't need to worry about us. I didn't want her to die worrying about us, I wanted her to find peace.

Exactly ninety three days after Grace went to the doctor and received her diagnosis, my wife died in my arms. Whispering our 'I love yous' until she took her very last breath and my whole world stopped. I'd never felt such soul crushing agony and I know I'd never feel anything like that again. I was broken, completely and truly destroyed. I'd never known a pain like it. I felt like I'd never take another breath. It felt like a strong wind could knock me over and shatter me into a million pieces.

That day was two and a half years ago and my entire soul is just as destroyed now as it was back then. I could truly never believe that the pain would dull at all. If I didn't have Lucie, I don't think I would have survived. But that little girl is all I have, and I am all she has.

So I bury the pain, I hide it from my daughter but it's always there, eating away at my body, mind and soul.

# Chapter Five

## Hugh

My days are monotonous. It's like reliving Groundhog Day over and over again.

I am woken everyday at the arse crack of dawn, by my gorgeous girl so I can't complain too much about that part. Morning snuggles are the best time of the day.

We get ready for our day, argue over having to eat a healthy breakfast. Argue some more about why she has to get washed and dressed. More arguing ensues when she's asked to put her shoes and coat on. Why don't kids ever just get the memo that we have to do things just because we have to.

It's pretty frustrating when you are having to deal with it all on your own. My parents take Lucie overnight every Friday, just to give me a break. I think there's an ulterior motive there though. They are hoping that one day I might meet someone special and move on. Fat chance of that happening.

Once we are finally ready, I drop Lucie at pre-school and then spend the next eight hours working at the fire station and fending off Ace. I love that man like a brother but if he doesn't stop trying to set me up with every single woman in the village, I might just have to punch him in the face.

Every evening is spent feeding and bathing Lucie before finally getting her to bed. I cherish every single second we have together and I love her fiercely. But life is hard. Being a parent is hard, always questioning whether I'm doing the right thing is beyond exhausting.

My evenings are usually spent on the sofa with a beer while I call Grace's voice mail over and over again just to hear her voice. I know it's unhealthy, but sometimes it feels like she's the only person I can talk to. I'd do anything for just one more moment with her.

I never thought I'd lose her so soon, she was healthy and happy. Until she wasn't and then she was just gone. We were supposed to grow old together, have more babies together and enjoy a long life. But she's gone now and has been for two and a half years. It doesn't get any easier and it's these quiet moments in the evenings that I feel it the most. It breaks my heart that I let her leave.

I know deep down that it was out of my control but it was my job to protect her, it was my job to weather the hard times. I would have taken her place if I could have.

We created photo albums of our life together but it hurts my soul seeing memories of her. We should have taken more photos and experienced more things together. We were supposed to have a whole lifetime to create more memories. But it was stolen from us and we can never get that back.

The only night of the week when things are a little different is on Fridays. With Lucie at my parents, Ace drags me down to Jax's with the boys. Jax is Ace's brother and he owns the local pub in the village with his wife Piper.

Jax is an interesting guy, he started off as a male stripper, saved up his money and made his dreams come true to live and work in Meadowside. He's a good guy to be around and he's fiercely protective of his wife, their teenage daughter Posie and their son Albie.

I always longed for that. A beautiful and healthy wife and children I could dote on. Unfortunately that wasn't in the cards for me, but I have the most important person in my life, Lucie. She's all I need. It's me and her against the world.

"Daddy, Daddy, Daddy ...wake up Daddy". The cutest little voice was whispering in my ear, pulling me from sleep. I'm exhausted, I feel like I could sleep for an entire week. Life was kicking my arse. I worked nine to five at the local fire station, five days a week while Lucie is at pre-school or with my parents.

I'm extremely lucky and grateful that my parents live close by and are always eager to help me out. They are an absolute godsend. However, they aren't here to save me from the excruciatingly early mornings that my daughter seems to take great joy in. Most mornings she is up before the sun, ready and raring to go. My thirty two year old brain and body take a bit longer to rouse from sleep.

"Daddy, I know you're awake because you're smiling". I could hear the smile in her voice. I crack open my eyes and peek up to see the most beautiful little angel sitting on my chest, leaning down so close that her little face is only inches away from mine.

"Of course I'm smiling Lulu, I'm looking at the most beautiful girl in the world". The smile that spreads across her face could bring joy to the grumpiest of souls. Man did I love this girl. 'I hungry', Lucie tells me. "Time to see Trudie?".

Going for breakfast at Trudie's was mine and Lucie's Saturday morning treat, before Lucie spent an hour at her dance class. We went to Trudie's Cafe every single week, ordering the exact same meal every time. Trudie was an sweet older lady in her late sixties, she runs the café with her husband Mitch who is the chef. They adore Lucie and always set our table up especially for us. A table for two right in the corner of the café, with a colouring book, crayons and always with Lucie's favourite flowers in the vase in the middle. Daisies are Lucie's favourite, we had put them on her Mummy's grave every single week since Grace left us. She called them her Mummy's flowers.

"It is time Lulu, let's get up and get dressed and then we can head off to see Trudie. What colour do you think she might be wearing today?".

"Pink Pink!" Lucie shouted. Trudie signature fashion was that she always wore the brightest vintage style dresses which Lucie just loved. She thought she was the brightest and sweetest lady on the planet, I was inclined to agree with her. Trudie had looked out for us since she first met us when Lucie was around six months old. She's known our story since the beginning. Grace was so loved in the community, it was hard for everybody when she left us. Coming to Trudie's with Lucie was the highlight of my week, we hadn't missed a week yet, apart from when Lucie went away for the weekend with my parents. They liked to give me a break every now and then and Lucie loved her adventures with Nana and Pop. Even when Lucie was away, I still went to Trudie's by myself.

We live right in the centre of our little village, which means that we are within walking distance to everything we need. It's quiet here, peaceful and full of friendly faces who had lived here for most of their lives. It was rare that you saw a face that you didn't recognise. We are local to the village, but have recently moved into a new little cottage. It was time. Before Grace died I thought we would have lived in our house forever. But it hadn't felt like home any more since she passed. It was time for a fresh start, so we moved into a tiny three bed cottage. The front door was bright yellow as per Lucie's request. We had a huge garden out back, with a little stream right at the very end of the property. I loved sitting out there in the mornings with my coffee, watching Lucie chasing butterflies or checking on her vegetables everyday. Lucie loved to help me cook, my mum had helped her to start her very own vegetable patch out in the garden and Lucie loved being able to grow and then cook her own veggies.

We said our hellos to people as we walked down the high street hand in hand, past the supermarket, the fire station, the local pub Jax's and the small library that sat at the opposite end of the road to Trudie's.

I opened the door for my little girl who shouted "Ding!" as she stepped over the threshold. Trudie had a little bell that rings whenever the door is opened. Kids have it so easy don't they, finding the simple pleasures in life. Lucie's shout always announces our arrival, prompting Trudie to come sweeping over to us and what do you know, she's wearing a pink dress.

"Good morning my lovelies, how're you doing today?" Trudie asks with a smile.

"We good," Lucie tells her. "We here for the pancakes!".

"Of course you are little Lucie, your table is all ready for you sweetie". Lucie leads the way through the café like she owns the place, saying good morning to all the customers she passes. She really is a little ray of sunshine, if only some of that sunshine could rub off on me.

We take our seats, Lucie already armed with her crayons and going to town on her colouring book.

"We have a new waitress that started just this week, she is from out of town, sweet and shy and looking for a fresh start. Now, don't you scare her away with your grumps will you?". She points at me raising a brow.

"Of course I won't Trudie, best behaviour I promise".

At that moment, I look behind Trudie to see the most beautiful woman walking towards us, she was tiny, much shorter than me. I'd say maybe 5'1 to my 6'3, gorgeous chocolate brown wavy hair pulled back in a ponytail. Curvy in all the right places but that wasn't the thing that drew me to her. It was her eyes, green, the same green as the stems of the daisies on our table, framed by long thick eyelashes fanning out across her cheeks. She slowly approached the table, waiting until the very last second to look up and make eye contact and when she did, she took my breath away. Not only were her eyes the most beautiful green I'd ever seen, but they were also the saddest eyes I'd seen in a long time. Not including when I looked at my reflection in the mirror.

# Chapter Six

## Sophie

Woah, blue eyes. The most gorgeous blue eyes I've ever seen. A blue that matches the colour of a summer sky. I've just come face to face with maybe the most beautiful man I've ever seen in my life. You know when you see something truly beautiful for the first time and the air leaves your lungs and you feel like you need to pick your jaw up off the floor. Yep, that's happening right now.

As I approach the table where he sits with a little girl. The beauty of a man stands and holds out his hand to me, I can't help but have to crane my neck up to meet his eyes. This man is tall, like really really tall. He has dark brown hair, cropped shorter on the sides and effortlessly longer messy strands on the top. He has a short stubbly beard across his masculine jaw, thick tattooed forearms shown off by his shirt sleeves rolled up to his elbows. Did I mention that he is utterly gorgeous! Muscles upon muscles upon muscles.

*Get yourself together Sophie, you're swooning in the middle of your brand new job!*

Once I've managed to unfreeze myself and get myself somewhat under control. I catch what he's just said in his deep velvety voice,

"Hi, I'm Hugh and this here is my daughter Lucie". I lean forward to shake his hand and as soon as our fingers touch, I feel the warm zap of electricity shoot up my arm. Woah what was that? I wonder if he felt it too?

*Respond to the man Sophie, you're making yourself look like an idiot!*

"Uh, Hi Hugh. It's very nice to meet you. And hi to you too Lucie, I love your colouring," I give Hugh's daughter a little wave. "I'm Sophie".

Hugh takes his seat again with a small smile. At that moment I realise that Trudie has left us and I remember that I actually have a job to do.

"So, what can I get you two on this early Saturday morning?"

"Two orders of pancakes with syrup please, coffee for me and an orange juice for this little one". Hugh strokes his daughters hair tenderly before turning back to me.

"Of course, I'll get that for you now".

A small head nod from Hugh and I turn away and hurry back around the counter. I busy myself with the coffee machine and take out a pink kiddies cup for Lucie's juice when Trudie appears around the corner with a kind but devious smile on her face. *Hmm I wonder what that's about.*

Soon enough the pancakes are ready and I deliver them to the table quickly. Hugh and I don't say anything more to one another for the remainder of his visit, aside from the usual waitress/customer pleasantries of course.

Within forty five minutes Hugh and Lucie are finished and on their way towards the door. Lucie leading the way of course, that little girl is so cute and confident. The way she announced her arrival earlier on made me smile so wide. Kids truly are a joy, they see life through a unique lens and they have no filter. I hope I do have one of my own one day, maybe I should see a doctor. What if there's something wrong with me?

I turn away to keep myself looking busy, but I can't help sneaking a peek at that fine man as he walks past towards the door.

I look up just as he does, *Busted!* I give him a small smile and wish him a good day. Just as I turn away, I feel a small tug at the apron tied around my waist. I look down to see Lucie smiling up at me, she cant be any more than three or four years old. She's adorable. I bend down to her eye level, "Hi Lucie, how can I help you sweet pea?" She places a piece of paper in my hand, "I made you a picture". I look down to see the cutest little drawing of a rainbow and three figures holding hands, she's even tried to sign her name too. "Wow Lucie, this is just amazing. I love it so much thank you. I think I'm going to stick it straight on my fridge when I get home". Just as I'm about to move to stand, she reaches for my hand "Your welcome, I hope it makes your eyes happy," with that she turns back and reaches for her Dad's hand. Hugh is stood frozen watching our conversation, it isn't until Lucie grabs his hand that he seems to come back to himself. See, kids have no filter. I wonder what she could see on my face that I've been trying so desperately to hide from the outside world. Obviously I haven't been doing a very good job.

"That was very kind Lucie, we will see you again soon Sophie," with that, they're gone. I'm frozen to the spot for a second, I wonder what she meant by that.

The rest of the day goes by in a flash and before I know it my shift is over and I'm on my way out of the door.

It's been exactly three weeks since I left Liam after finding out about his affair and to be honest I'm not much better off now than I was then emotionally. That night I hopped into my car with my two suitcases and just drove. I had no destination in mind, I didn't even pay attention to where I was heading, it's a miracle I made it in one piece really. I just left. I slept in my car that night, for the first time in my life I was so incredibly broken that I didn't even care. I would have slept on a park bench if that was the only choice.

I drove around for two whole days before I felt the urge to stop and find somewhere a little more comfortable to lay my head. I pulled into a little village called Meadowside, found myself a hotel and wallowed in my misery for the next week after that. I barely ate or showered, I couldn't even bring myself to get out of bed.

Somehow I managed to find enough strength to get out of bed eventually and have a look around. I found myself at Trudie's and the rest is history. I'm pretty sure she could see something in me that called to her.

She seems like the motherly type who would do anything to help somebody in need. Not only did she give me a job working at the café but she's also letting me stay in the tiny studio apartment above the café, rent free. All I have to pay for is my utilities and groceries.

I let myself into the apartment and head straight for the bedroom. Stripping of my greasy smelling uniform and changing into my comfy leggings and hoodie. I don't need to worry about what I look like, it's not as if anybody is going to come knocking at the door. Nobody knows me here, nobody is looking for me. Liam was the only family I had, apart from a few girlfriends but they weren't real friends, just acquaintances who were in a similar situation to me. They were the wives of Liam's partners at the law firm and I can't even bring myself to want anything to do with any of them.

*Did they know? They must have seen Liam's relationship change with his 'client'.*

I'm a thirty two year old woman and I'm not at all ashamed to say I want my Mum, I wish she was here. Just for a hug. I lost my parents years ago, they were older parents and didn't have me until they were well into their forties. They both died relatively young. I'd do anything for a hug from them. My Mum would know just what to say to help me put myself back together again.

My entire live has imploded, it feels like I'm trapped in hell but I can't find the door. I can't find a way out, can't take a breath. I don't know what to do next. So, for now I'll work at Trudie's and come home to my empty, cold apartment all by myself.

The only positive to being chronically lonely, epically heartbroken and with all this extra time on hands is that I've been writing loads. The words seem to pouring out of me. They say you write from your heart, from things you've experienced yourself. I'm always so trapped inside my head, have been for a long time, always felt so alone. The difference is that now I actually am alone.

# Chapter Seven

**Hugh**

*Dear Sweetheart,*
*Lucie woke me up at the crack of dawn again today, God that*
*kid has your love of early mornings. Would it hurt her to have*
*a lie in every now and then?! She really is the sweetest little*
*thing though, you'd be so proud of her.*
*She done great in her little ballet class today, followed all the*
*steps and looked adorable in her little pink leotard and tutu.*
*Shame she seems to have inherited my lack of rhythm though.*
*Poor kid!*
*We ate breakfast at Trudie's again this morning, like every*
*week. Syrup and pancakes all round of course. Just the thought*
*of them makes me feel a little sick, as you know I'm not the*
*greatest lover of them. But Lucie insists, so how could I ever*
*say no?*

*Trudie has a new waitress that started this week. Her name is Sophie. She seems sweet and quiet. She seems like a broken soul, a bit like me.*
*She has the most beautiful sad green eyes. When we shook hands I felt something. A warmth, a tingle ... something. I've not had any sort of reaction to another woman since you left, it's taken me by surprise.*
*Is that ok?*
*I'll write again soon my love,*
*Your Hugh x*

Lucie's fourth birthday is coming up soon, I can't believe she's turning four. It's gone so incredibly fast, I feel like I've blinked and just like that she's not my tiny baby any more. She's adorable, sweet, thoughtful and has a sassy side which makes me dread her teenage years!

She's asked for a tea party with all her little friends from pre-school. I've managed to arrange that with Trudie. She's closing down the café just for Lucie. She's making the food and cake. I've booked a face painter, mini DJ set up and a storytelling session with my buddy Ace's girlfriend Lily. Lily is the librarian at the library in the village, she's planning to tell some stories and get the kids involved. Lucie is a massive bookworm so she's going to really love it. Fingers crossed.

Birthdays are always tricky without Grace here, it makes me realise how much she's missing. Lucie was only 15 months when we lost her Mum. Grace only got to be there for her first birthday and then we lost her a few months later. I feel like I have to make special occasions even more special for Lucie, as she only has me. I feel like I have to make up for what she's lost. Of course, she knows no different. It's heart-breaking that she doesn't remember her Mum, but I also think that may be a small blessing in disguise. It doesn't cause her the pain that it causes me.

Monday is here again and that means it's off to work for me. Lucie is at pre-school today so once I've dropped her off I make my way over to the station.

"Hey Buddy, good weekend?" Ace says the minute I walk through the door. I swear this guy misses nothing. He's like a hound sniffing things out before they've even happened.

"Mornin' man, all good thanks, breakfast with Lucie at Trudie's on Saturday like usual and then spent the day yesterday at the house playing with Lucie". I couldn't help but think of Sophie and those beautiful green eyes as soon as I mentioned Trudie's. To be honest she'd been on my mind more than I'd care to admit since we met. Ace being the sniffer dog that he is, noticed whatever flashed across my face at that moment. I couldn't help but roll my eyes heavenward before the inquisition began.

"Hmm, breakfast you say, anything interesting happen at all?". His eyebrows couldn't get any closer to his hairline if he tried.

"Nope, nothing at all. Pancakes, coffee, dance class then home time". I started putting my things into my locker and got changed into my uniform, getting ready in case we get a call . I was also trying to make myself look incredibly busy so that Ace may take the hint and move along to bug someone else. Don't get me wrong, I love the guy. He's a good friend and a real good time when we go out to the pub but he's like a dog with a bone and doesn't seem to have an off switch.

"Mmm hmm". Ace looked as though he knew exactly what or who I'd met. He was the most confident person I'd ever met, he didn't walk he swaggered. He also never stopped talking which was why I was surprised that he didn't say anything more about it.

I quickly changed the subject and got stuck into work. It was a relatively quiet morning until lunchtime came around and Ace was walking towards me like a man on a mission, laser focused on my face with a mischievous glint in his eye.

"Nope, nuh uh, not happening," I managed to choke out before he'd even said a word. I could read this man like a book, we'd known each other since school. We had grown up together, he couldn't get his antics past me.

"Don't know what you mean man, me and the guys are just heading to Trudie's for lunch and we think you should come along and join us. They make the best bacon butties in town". Ace bit his lip to hold back his grin. He wasn't fooling me. I opened my mouth to respond, but before I'd even had a chance to come up with an excuse I was surrounded. Ace to my left with his arm around my shoulders, Ryan to my right holding back his own smile and Mack behind me edging me along towards the door.

Looks like I wasn't getting out of this after all.

# Chapter Eight

## Sophie

It had been a quiet morning at Trudie's so far. That wouldn't last long as the lunchtime rush was about to start. I'd spent the morning in the kitchen with Mitch, he had just discovered my love of baking and would not let me leave the kitchen until I'd made three cakes to display on the counter for our customers.

Mitch was a man of very few words I'd come to learn, so I figured I'd humour the old man and spend some time hanging out in the kitchen with him. I would never admit just how much I had loved being back in the kitchen. My mum had taught me all of her baking recipes while I was growing up and it was our favourite thing to do together, my dad was designated taste tester of course. I even had them all written up neatly in a recipe book at home. I kept hold of it, it was a prized possession. I always hoped to one day use it to teach my own children how to bake. Well, as we all know, that panned out well didn't it.

Trudie of course had to taste test all three, concluding that the chocolate brownie cake was her firm favourite. With my coffee and walnut cake coming in second and the red velvet cupcakes a very close third. Watching her and Mitch try my cakes brought a happiness to my heart that I haven't felt for a very long time. We were still laughing and smiling when the door flew open and in swept four, yes four, gorgeous firefighters. *Oh boy, it was getting hot in here!*

One guy stepped forward, he was tall with messy brown hair, a stubbled jaw and big brown eyes. He looked like one of those models you'd see on a billboard flashing his underwear and washboard abs! "Why hello there cutie, we would like a table for four please" *I don't think a table for four was going to be big enough, these guys were huge!*

"No problem," I said with a smile as I grabbed some menus and led them towards an open booth big enough for the giant hotties to fit in. They stepped past one by one, nodding their heads and muttering their greetings to me. *One giant hottie, two giant hotties, three giant hotties.* The fourth guy was just moving past when I caught the most gorgeous whiff of cologne, man and soap mixed together. I lifted my eyes and got immediately swept up in the most beautiful blue eyes. I knew those eyes, I'd been dreaming of them for the past few nights. *Four giant hotties.*

"Hi Sophie, nice to see you again," Hugh said quietly with warmth in his voice and a sweet smile of his face. His chest brushed mine as he squeezed past me to his seat, I caught his deep inhale of breath. He looked as shocked as I was as he caught mine. My nipples were hard points in my bra and a shiver worked down my whole body. *Holy moly I'm in trouble here, what was it with this man?*

Once they were settled, they placed their food and drink orders and I got back to work. If I kept myself busy enough then I would forget he was here right? Wrong! I could feel eyes on me as I moved around the café, it was burning a flush of heat down my spine and I was getting hotter and hotter by the second. I lifted my head to check on the other customers and tried to keep myself from looking in Hugh's direction.

We were like magnets, drawn to each other, I looked over and our eyes clashed. I couldn't quite make out the emotion in his eyes. Was it pain, guilt, heat, lust? I knew what I was feeling and if I didn't excuse myself in the next ten seconds I was going to spontaneously combust right here in the middle of a busy café at lunchtime.

"Trudie, I'm just taking a quick bathroom break," I called as I practically sprinted down the corridor to the bathrooms. I pushed open the door and hurried straight to the sink to splash cold water on my face, "Get a grip Soph, he's just a man, you've given up on them remember!". I stared at myself in the mirror, I was so flushed I looked like I'd been standing directly in the sun! I gave myself a few minutes to cool off before I wiped my sweaty palms down my apron, took a deep breath, held my head up high and headed out the door and walked smack bang into the hardest wall of muscle I'd ever felt.

"Oh my God, I'm so sorry sir," I blurted out before the smell of man and soap assaulted my senses and I lifted my eyes and was held hostage by those beautiful blues. We were standing so close to one another that I would only have to slightly rise and our lips would be pressed together. Neither of us seemed in any hurry to move apart, it was as if we were in another dimension, frozen, unblinking as we just stared at each other. Hugh's huge, warm hands held on tightly to the tops of my arms. He was breathing hard, as hard as I was. His eyes looked pained and intense. I couldn't look away, we were in our own little world and nobody else seemed to exist. Time stood still.

"Sophie!" Trudie called from the kitchen and in an instant the spell was broken. In sync we both took a step backwards, a small smile on Hugh's face as he whispered "Sorry Soph," and headed back towards his seat. *Why did him calling me 'Soph' make my heart do that little pitter patter thing? Oh man, this was bad. Was I so deprived of male attention that the shortening of my name had me practically ready to climb this man like a tree and grind against his hard body!*

I hurried into the kitchen, turned and leaned my back against the door as it closed. My heart was pounding and I felt like I had little hearts bursting out of my eyes. Trudie stuck her head out from behind the oven, "The hottie table want some slices of cake

Sophie, I told them that you'd baked them fresh this morning. They'd like two slices of each and four cupcakes to takeaway".

"Oh ... oh okay sure". I headed back out into the café and went about slicing up the cake and putting the cupcakes into a to go box. I carried them all over to the table on a tray and set it down.

"Oh my God look at that cake," the guy called Ace muttered with a groan. The guy I'd learnt was called Ryan just stared at the cake, visibly salivating. He was like a big friendly golden retriever, I'd totally just made his day with a slice of cake. I couldn't help but giggle. The third man, Mack, I think he was called snapped his hands forward quickly grabbing a slice of chocolate brownie cake "Mine!".

Hugh huffed out a laugh and pulled the last plate of coffee and walnut cake towards him, I couldn't take my eyes off of him. For some reason I wanted his approval, hoping he would like it. He speared a piece with his fork and brought it to his lips, his very nice firm lips I might add. He chewed and chewed, I couldn't help but watch his Adams apple bob as his swallowed. He wasn't giving anything away, he definitely wasn't as animated as his friends. I wasn't prepared for the next sound to leave his mouth. He moaned, he literally moaned, a deep groan sounding from his throat, "Ohhh ..... Sophie, this is divine". I nearly groaned along with him, heat rushed down my body to between my legs, I could feel my heartbeat throbbing there. *God, I know it's been a loooooong time since I had some good sex but really, the man is eating cake!*

I was fully aware that I needed to pick my jaw up off the floor and say something, anything. But it wasn't until Ace nudged me that I was brought back into the room. He looked at me with a smirk on his pretty face and his eyebrows raised. I could feel the flush working it's way up my neck to my face. I felt like I was as red as a tomato!

"Oh, erm I'm really glad you all like it. My Mum taught me to bake when I was younger. It's been a while..." I trailed off. Talking about my Mum always hurt my heart just a little. Changing subject I said "I've put a couple of extra cupcakes in here for your little girl Hugh. I hope she likes them".

"Ah, thanks. She will love them, that girl has the biggest sweet tooth of anyone I've met. I'll be sure to let her know that they're from you". He said with a smile and turned back to finish his slice of cake.

"You're welcome. Have a good afternoon guys". I said as the guys all finished their cake in record time, stood, throwing their cash on the table and getting ready to move towards the door. I began to clean up their table and collect their cash when a warm hand closed around my elbow and Hugh's deep voice sounded close to my ear, "Thank you again for the cupcakes Soph. It was great to see you again, you're a really talented baker". He gave me a sweet, sexy smile. A squeeze of my elbow and he was gone.

I could have melted to the floor right then and there, I needed to get new batteries for my vibrator and pronto!

# Chapter Nine

**Sophie**

Friday rolled around before I knew it and I had a half day at the café today, which meant that I was finished by one o'clock and was ready to head home. I didn't fancy spending the next eighteen hours locked away in my apartment before my next shift at the café so I decided to have a wander down the high street. I haven't explored much since I got here, the only place I'd been to was the grocery store.

This village really was a lovely place, picturesque really. All of the little shops had flower boxes on their windows ledges and benches outside where people chatted and caught up with their neighbours. Everybody seemed to know each other, but everybody was really friendly and I got lots of "good afternoons" as I walked past. I walked to the very end of the road, I'd been in a few shops and brought a few little homey knick knacks for my apartment. I didn't really need anything but it's always nice to add a little something of yourself to a new home and I'd left all of my belongings back home with Liam. Everything apart from my clothes of course.

I noticed the fire station up ahead and couldn't help but slow my walk like an absolute creeper. I wondered if Hugh was working today. I decided on a bench across the street, it seemed like a nice enough place to eat my sandwich that Trudie had sent me home with. This wasn't suspicious right? I was just sat on the bench eating my lunch, minding my own business.

Movement caught my eye and in a flash a group of fire-fighters came dashing around the corner, scrambling to put on their fire jackets and helmets. My eyes were drawn immediately to Hugh, I mean he's pretty hard to miss. He's huge and towered over the other guys. He climbed into the cab of the fire engine, looked like he was the driver. All the other guys scrambled in alongside him and then they were off. Siren blaring, lights flashing as he pulled up to the road. His eyes caught mine and the sexiest smirk lifted the corner of his mouth, he recognised me immediately. He raised a hand in a manly wave before they tore off down the road. I didn't just have butterflies in my stomach, they were like giant pterodactyls trying to burst out of my body. I've never had a reaction like this to a man before, not even my husband.

I was heading back down the high street when I came across a tiny little library. It was set back from the rest of the buildings. It was painted light pink, with flowers outside in hanging baskets. It might be the cutest little place I'd ever seen. I couldn't help myself as I headed towards the door. I felt like I was heading into Snow White's little cottage with the dwarves, something about it felt magical. I pulled open the door and the smell of old books hit me instantly, I had forgotten about my love of them with all the recent drama in my life.

I headed inside and started up and down the aisles, stroking my fingers over the spines of the books. I could see myself spending a lot of time here. There was a little children's nook in the corner, decorated in bright colours with cartoon characters adorning the walls. A big fluffy rug sat in the middle with what looked like a little story time session starting. Small children and their parents were gathered on the rug listening to a story about a bear and his animal friends. Happy ever after guaranteed of course.

I carried on exploring and found a little nook for the adults too, a few tables pushed into the middle and a couple of large comfy sofas against the wall. It seemed like the perfect place to curl up with a book. *Or maybe write one.* I could see myself working here. I decided there and then that I'd come back with my laptop one day. I finished at the café by four o'clock most days and the library was open until seven in the evening.

I made my way up to the counter with the small selection of books I'd collected whilst wandering. The lady that I'd seen leading the children's story time session was finished and stood behind the counter with a huge smile on her face. I could tell just by looking at her that she was sunshine in human form. She seemed sweet and happy and immediately welcomed me,

"Hi! Welcome to Meadowside Library. My names' Lily, it's so lovely to meet you. I've seen you at Trudie's. You must be Sophie". Wow, I'd never been 'known' anywhere, usually I just disappeared into the crowd or was completely invisible.

"Uh hi Lily, yep that's me. I recently moved to the village and Trudie has been so kind in helping me out while I get settled. It's lovely to meet you Lily". I proceeded to place my books on the counter and asked if I could borrow them.

"You know, me and my girlfriends are heading over to Jax's tonight. You know, the pub on the corner. I'd love it if you'd join us?" She looked at me with hope in her eyes. I couldn't understand why she was being so kind, nobody ever showed me much attention.

"Oh erm, I'm not sure. You don't know me, I'd hate to crash your time with your friends". I was flustered, fumbling for an excuse to go home and hide.

Lily looked at me with a sweet smile and lent across to rest her small hand on my arm.

"You're new to town, we don't get many newbies show up here. We would love it if you'd join us. We can give you all the small town gossip!". She really seemed to want me to go. Maybe I should. I'd been here for weeks and barely left the café or the apartment. What was the harm in trying to make a few friends while I was here.

Screw it, I was going to go for it.

"Well if you're sure, I'd love to join you. I haven't made any friends here yet. What time should I meet you?".

Once we had arranged a time to meet and Lily had checked out my books to borrow I decided to head home and procrastinate about tonight. I waved goodbye to Lily and headed home. What was I going to wear? What were we going to talk about?

What were the chances that perhaps Hugh would be there? There was only one pub in town and it was Friday night after all. I didn't even know if he was single for goodness sake, well obviously not, he had a small child. Chances are he was married and I had just gotten out of a ten year marriage. I needed to shut this down. Tonight was about making friends and nothing more.

# Chapter Ten

## Sophie

I walked into the pub exactly at seven in the evening. I had spent hours trying to come up with an excuse not to go, trying to talk myself out of going and then trying to talk myself back into going. In the end, I decided it would be rude to just not turn up. I didn't even have Lily's number so I wouldn't have been able to let her know I wasn't coming anyway.

I made a deal with myself, I had to stay for one hour and then I could make my excuses and head home.

I spotted Lily straight away, she was a tiny little thing. Short and petite with icy blonde hair and thick framed glasses. She was sat at a table in the corner of the room with two other women. One was a gorgeous brunette with slightly wavy hair. She looked like she had come straight from a shift at the hospital, dressed in blue scrubs. The other woman was a red head and I could tell just by looking at her that she was going to be fun. She had this mischievous, feisty glint in her eye. They welcomed me as soon as I walked towards the table, you wouldn't think that we were only just meeting for the first time. All three stood up and gave me a hug. The brunette introduced herself as Freya and the red head was Maisie. I felt at ease immediately.

We spent a few minutes making small talk and getting to know each other before ordering our first round of drinks. I'm not a big drinker but had decided to let my hair down, after spending the entire afternoon worrying about tonight it was safe to say that I was in need of some liquid courage. The others told me a little bit about themselves. Freya was a paediatric nurse who worked in the local hospital. She had a boyfriend called Ryan who was a fire-fighter. It didn't take me long to figure out that I'd already met him back in the café. He was the guy drooling over my cake! I couldn't help but laugh and so did Freya when I told her I'd already met her partner. "Yep that sounds about right for Ryan, he's a huge child and just cannot help himself". We all laughed along with her.

Maisie was the local vet, and I was totally right with my first impressions of her. She was funny, flirty and feisty. I wouldn't want to get on her bad side, I could tell you that right now. She had been married to her husband Mack for five years and he was also a fire-fighter. The other cake loving fire-fighter that I'd met at the café. "He was incredibly possessive over his slice of chocolate cake". I couldn't wipe the smile off my face. I felt like I'd known these ladies for years, rather than just minutes.

"Oh believe me," Maisie said with a smirk, "That is not the only thing he is possessive of! He hates me coming here on a Friday night. For some reason he thinks we just sit here getting hit on the entire night. He knows the whole place is full of old cronies and he knows every single one of them by name". She said with an eye roll.

Before Lily could tell me about herself, I took the chance to hazard a guess, "I'm going to take a guess and say that your fella is called Ace?" I asked with a smile, Lily nodded with little love hearts in her eyes. "He was very sweet when he came to the café, he made sure to make me feel welcome in town. He's also very charismatic".

"Oh tell me about it, that man flirts with peoples grandmas! He literally cannot help himself. I'm pretty sure it's just built into his DNA and he couldn't stop if he tried. He's harmless though, he's incredibly loyal and would do absolutely anything for anyone". I could tell that when I met him. He seemed like an incredibly nice guy, flirty, charismatic and completely harmless.

I couldn't help the question that blurted out of my mouth next, it must have been the alcohol that had loosened me up a bit.

"What about Hugh? Is there not a lady missing from your little group?". The group instantly turned sombre and I couldn't help but feel like I'd said something wrong. I backtracked quickly, "Oh no, never mind. I shouldn't have asked. I didn't mean to pry".

It was Freya that spoke up, she looked to the other ladies, took a breath and then said quietly, "Yeah, there's someone missing. Hugh is my brother in law. He was married to my sister Grace".

"What do you mean, was? Where is she now?". I asked, trying to be delicate. I had a feeling that we'd just stepped into bad territory. I wish I'd never brought up Hugh in the first place.

"Erm, Grace died almost three years ago," Freya whispered. I could see the emotion welling in her eyes. Lily and Maisie scooted closer to her on either side and I couldn't stop myself from reaching across the table and taking her hand in mine.

"I'm so sorry for your loss Freya and I'm so sorry I asked. You don't have to tell me any more".

"No, no it's fine. It's just difficult to talk about, it happened so quickly and it feels like just yesterday that we lost her. Grace was diagnosed with stage four cancer when Lucie was just a baby. Lucie is my niece, she's about the turn four next week". She said with a smile.

"I've met Lucie, she came to the café with Hugh last Saturday. She's such a sweetheart, she drew me a picture. I have it stuck on my fridge at home," I said with a smile and squeezed Freya's hand.

She laughed, and the love for Lucie shone in her eyes. "She's adorable, she looks just like Grace. She reminds me so much of her, she's sweet, kind, loving .... a little sassy".

"It's been a really hard couple of years, especially for Hugh. He's raising that little girl all by himself, while grieving for Grace. He has his parents close by though, and we all help out as much as we can. Lucie doesn't remember Grace. She's started asking about her more and more as she's getting older. It's so heart breaking.

Grace would be so incredibly proud of her, and Hugh too. He's really stepped up. He's one of the best men I know". I didn't even know what to say, all I could offer Freya was a kind smile. I stood up from my chair and went round to give her a hug.

"Right, that's enough of all that," Maisie said with a giggle. "No more tears, tonight is meant to be for fun and getting to know our new friend. So, Sophie tell us about yourself. What brings you to our tiny town?".

I huffed out a laugh as I took my seat again, nothing about my story was funny. I felt I could open up though and tell them. Freya had just told me all about losing her sister. I could tell them about my cheating piece of shit husband.

I took a deep breath and the word vomit spewed out of me. I told them all about my marriage, that I'd always felt alone, unsupported and kind of just forgotten about. Then I told them about the recent events that led to me leaving Liam and ending up here.

"Holy shit, what an absolute arsehole!" Maisie shouted loud enough for us to attract a few funny looks. Lily and Freya were just gaping at me. I think I'd shocked them. I mean, it was a pretty shocking story.

I shrugged my shoulders, reached for my drink and downed it in one. Maisie shouted to Jax the bartender, "We need more drinks ... pronto! Just bring the whole bottle". I couldn't help but laugh out loud, I sounded almost hysterical. I laughed so hard that they quickly turned into tears. I hadn't let myself truly break down and cry about it all in weeks and now the flood gates had opened I couldn't seem to stop. My new friends were up and by my side in seconds, all three of them. I was surrounded by love, I'd never had real friends before but I felt like I'd found them now. After a few minutes of hugs and love, I felt like a weight had been lifted off my shoulders. I'd told somebody my story, they didn't judge me. They didn't tell me that it was my fault. They listened, they cared. I felt like I could finally breathe.

Maisie filled our glasses again from the bottle in the middle of the table, "A toast," she said and held her glass high, we all did the same and waited for her toast, "To divorcing selfish arseholes," she said with a laugh. We all burst into a fit of giggles. It wasn't until we heard a throat clearing that we realised we were no longer alone.

"Errr Mais, why are you talking about divorcing arseholes? I know I can be a bit of a dick sometimes but you're not leaving me. I'm not letting you go". It was Mack, standing next to our table with a scowl on his face. Ace, Ryan and Hugh were all standing behind him, looking to be holding back their laughter. Of course, Ace was the first one to bend over howling with laughter. The rest of us couldn't help but laugh along with him. Maisie got up and went to console her husband, "You are a dick babe, but you're my dick and I love you ... and your dick!" She gave her eyebrows a waggle and the look of relief on Mack's face almost set us all off again.

"So, can we join you lovely ladies?" Ace asked, scooting in next to Lily before anyone had even answered, once he had recovered from laughing so hard of course. He swung his arm around her shoulders and gave her a kiss that definitely was not appropriate with an audience.

The other guys all scooted in next to their partners, leaving the only open seat next to me. Hugh gave Freya a kiss on her cheek with a whispered "Hey Fifi," and ruffled her hair like a little kid. He sat down next to me. It was getting so crowded around our table now that we were pressed together, touching from knee to shoulder.

I just sat ramrod straight, engulfed in his gorgeous scent. Clinging to my drink like it was a life raft. I felt so compassionate towards him now that I knew his story, that didn't stop me swooning and melting into a puddle in my seat. It was getting busy in the pub, the noise level had gone up a notch. Hugh lent close to my ear, I could feel his warm breath on my neck which sent a shiver down my spine before he shouted "Hey Soph, good to see you. How are you doing?".

I'd never been so nervous around a man before. There go those damn pterodactyls again!

# Hugh

She seems nervous around me. I couldn't figure out why. I really hope I don't make her feel uncomfortable. It's been such a long time since I sat next to a woman and got to know her. She leaned close to my ear and the scent of raspberries and vanilla assaulted my senses, wow she smells good enough to eat. She spoke so softly in my ear "Hi Hugh, it's so nice to see you too. I'm fine thank you, how are you?".

"I'm good thanks, Lucie is at my parents for the night so I'm hanging with these hooligans. They pretty much forced me to come out, but the night is starting to look up a little bit". She gave me a sweet smile and I watched the blush creep up her neck to her cheeks.

We spend the next hour or so getting to know each other a little better, nothing too heavy, just some small talk. Turns out she loves working for Trudie, loves to read and spends most of her time at home. I'm trying to work up the courage to ask her story. When me and the guys arrived at the pub we overheard Maisie shouting about divorce and Sophie's eyes looked a little red as if she'd been crying. Mack had a little panic, it was hilarious, as if those two would ever divorce. I've never met two people more perfect for each other.

"So, I hope you don't think I'm too forward in asking and please do tell me to shut the hell up if you want to. What was the whole 'divorcing arseholes' thing about?". Sophie looked down into her drink like it's the most interesting thing in the world, for a long time I don't think she's going to answer me. But then she lifts her eyes, a world of pain in them and tells me her story, "Well, erm, I moved here very recently, about four or five weeks ago now. I moved here because, well because I left my husband after I found out he'd been having an affair for the better part of a year. Not only that, but he got her pregnant too. We had been trying to have a baby for a long time but it never happened. Now, I'm beginning to think that maybe it didn't happen for a reason. Like maybe fate was trying to tell me that it wasn't right. Who knows. And now I'm going to shut up because I just spewed word vomit all over you". She looked back down into her drink. I've never heard her speak so many words in one go. I'm momentarily shocked and at a total loss for words. What am I meant to say to that.

"I'm so sorry, I didn't mean to tell you all of that".

I hold up my hand to stop her, "Sophie, I ... I don't really know what to say. What an absolute arsehole. I mean how could he do that. He has the most beautiful woman in the world as his wife and he just throws her away just like that!". Ah man, I said too much. I mentally face palm.

Sophie just looks at me in shock, "You think I'm beautiful?" She whispers, it's so loud in here that I can't hear her but I can tell that's what she just said.

I lean in close to her ear again, "Fancy going for a walk? We can't talk properly here and I'd really love to be able to hear you when I'm getting to know you". I smirk at her, there goes that blush again. She places her drink down and gives me a little nod.

We say goodbye to our friends, telling them that I'm going to walk Sophie home. I give Freya a kiss on her head, she grabs my hand hard and gives it a squeeze. She looks deep into my eyes and gives me a nod and smile. She looks so much like Grace it's uncanny. I think that's her way of telling me it's ok to get to know Sophie.

We leave the pub and as soon as we walk outside it's like a true breath of fresh air.

"Wow that's better, I can hear myself think again". I look over to Sophie and she's just looking at me with the most beautiful smile on her face. I'm very much aware of the fact that I didn't answer her question about whether I think she's beautiful. Of course she is, has she never looked in the mirror. She's absolutely stunning, something is holding me back from telling her that though.

I know Grace begged me on her death bed to move on one day. She told me it was ok to feel again one day but I never truly thought that day would come. I love my wife and always will. She owns my heart, even though she isn't here any more to claim it. However, I haven't been tempted in the slightest to get to know anybody. Not until I met Sophie in the café that day with Lucie.

We begin to walk down the high street in the direction of Trudie's when Sophie asks, "How's Lucie doing?".

"Ah she's great. Thanks for asking. It's her birthday next week and I haven't heard the end of it. We are having a party at Trudie's next Saturday and she keeps adding more and more things that she would like to do. I may have to re mortgage the house just for this party! She's the sassiest almost four year old I've ever met". I can't help but feel a burst of pride though just thinking about Lucie. She may be sassy and she may exhaust me beyond belief but I wouldn't change a single thing about her.

"I heard she was having a birthday party. Trudie has actually asked me to make her birthday cake," she looks up shyly at me. She's so much shorter than me, she almost has to crane her neck all the way back.

"What's her favourite flavour? Does she have a favourite colour?. I'd like to make it perfect for her".

"Well she loved those cupcakes you sent home for her, I didn't even get a taste! Her favourite colour is pink. Please don't worry too much though, whatever you make she will absolutely love. I'm so pleased you're making it, I wondered if Trudie would ask you to help". I look back at Sophie but she's already looking at me, she really does have the most beautiful eyes.

Time freezes and neither of us seems to be able to look away, we probably should have though because before I can even comprehend what's happened, Sophie is falling. I don't even think, I just grab her and haul her against my chest, her back to my front. I can feel her heart pounding against my arms which are wrapped around her from behind. She's breathing fast and so am I. I still haven't let go and she hasn't asked me to. My heart is pounding as my cock goes rock solid against her back. She's warm and soft and her curves are sinful. If she can feel me hard and pressed against her back she doesn't say anything. But then a small whimper escapes her lips and my cock throbs. Oh man, I need to let go. I slowly move my hands to the top of her arms and ask her barely above a whisper "Are you ok?". She's still breathing hard, I turn her to face me. She's blushing, mm mm what that blush does to me. I am rock solid and pressing so hard against my zipper it's almost painful. I really need to adjust myself but I can't do that without making it incredibly obvious.

As the thought crosses my mind, her eyes leave mine, they trail down my body going lower and lower. Her breath hitches, "Wow," she says, almost in awe. I can't help but lower my eyes too to see what she's staring at and boy oh boy, yep there's no hiding that. My t-shirt has ridden up and gotten caught in my belt, must have happened when I grabbed her. But that's not what has her saying wow. My cock is so hard that my tip is peeking out of the waistband of my jeans, not only that but it's glistening under the street lamp like a beacon saying "HELP, I HAVEN'T GOTTEN LAID IN OVER TWO YEARS!". Mentally face palm again. I reach down to adjust myself, Sophie is still standing so close I can smell her. It's not helping the rock solid situation we have going on down here. "I'm sorry," I whisper to her. She slowly raises her eyes to mine, yep they were still firmly on my rock solid cock.

"Oh, erm, I. There's nothing to be sorry about". She's breathless, almost panting. I need to get her home as fast as possible so I can go home and relieve this problem, it hurts. "Come on honey, let's get you home". With that we walk, almost run down the road towards Trudie's.

"I'm staying in the apartment above the café," Sophie clarifies before I ask. "She's so incredibly kind, she's looked out for me since I arrived in town". Trudie really is a good soul and from what I've learned about Sophie tonight she could do with some good friends in her life. Nothing like thinking of a sixty plus grandma to kill your boner though.

"Well I should head home, it was so nice to see you again. I really enjoyed getting to know you," I say with a smile, trying to play off the whole cock hanging out situation. If we don't talk about it, it didn't happen right?

"It was lovely to get to know you too Hugh, hopefully we can do it again sometime". Before I can stop myself I'm leaning forward and pressing my lips to Sophie's cheek. Her breath hitches and just like that, the boner is back.

# Chapter Eleven

**Hugh**

*Dear Sweetheart,*
*How have you been? Things here have gotten a little ... com-*
*plicated. I ran into Sophie down at the pub on Friday night*
*and spent some time getting to know her. She's really sweet*
*and she's been through such a terrible ordeal, totally explains*
*why she has such a sad look in her eyes.*
*I offered to walk her home and that's when things got a little*
*awkward. I reacted to her Grace, like in a way I haven't*
*reacted to anybody in such a long time. I feel like I need to*
*apologise to you, I know that probably seems silly, you're not*
*even here.*
*I think I like her Grace, like really like her. I suppose there's*
*no harm in a physical reaction right, it's not as if I'm going to*
*fall in love with her.*
*Right?*
*Love Always,*

## *Hugh x*

I blink open my eyes slowly, it's still dark outside. I glance at the clock on my bedside table, it's four o'clock on Tuesday morning. I know what's woken me up, as it's the same thing that's woken me for the past four nights. Something I've not acknowledged in the hope that it might just go way. But it's not working, I need to do something to get rid of this feeling.

I glance down at myself whilst laying in bed, letting out a frustrated sigh. My cock is so hard it's tenting the bedsheets.

Ahh man, I'm so hard that it's painful and it's the object of my sleeping problems since Friday night. I can't stop thinking about Sophie and how she felt in my arms, pressed up against me.

She's so god damn beautiful, her long brown wavy hair that I just want to wrap around my fist. Her beautiful green eyes that light up when she looks at me. Her scent, like fresh raspberries and vanilla. Her body is sinful, she's not stick thin, no she has beautiful curves, luscious firm tits and a gorgeous round arse that I want to sink my teeth into.

My hand moves as if it has a mind of it's own, I've been holding myself back but I just can't any more, I need to deal with this ... problem and move on.

I push my hand into my boxer briefs, taking my rock solid cock in my hand. I squeeze the base hard to try and relieve some pressure. It doesn't work. I let out an involuntary moan.

Pre-cum is already beading at my tip which I swipe away with my thumb.

I push my boxers down over my arse with my other hand and my cock springs free from it's tight restraints. Feels better already. I feel almost frantic. I close my eyes and give over to my urges, I'm only human after all and not doing anybody any harm.

I spit into my hand and reach down again to grip my dick hard and begin to move my hand up and down, stroking firmly. Yeah that feels good. Images of beautiful green eyes and chocolate brown hair flicker behind my eye lids. I imagine Sophie down on her knees between my legs. It's her hand gripping me tight, moving slowly but firmly, rubbing me up and down. She licks her lips whilst looking up at me and uses her thumb to wipe the bead of pre cum from my tip. Reaching up to swipe it across her tongue, she closes her eyes and hums out her approval.

She slowly leans forward and takes my rock hard, dripping cock between her lips, using her tongue to lick the veins on the underside. She takes me deep into her mouth, all the way to the back of her throat, she gags a little, which just makes this whole daydream even damn hotter.

I gather her hair in my hand and wrap it around my wrist as she speeds up, I need to watch her taking my cock like the good girl she is. This is all happening in my mind of course, and I know that, it's my own hand going to town on my cock bringing me closer and closer to exploding into what I can already tell is going to be an epic orgasm.

But my mind is making it feel so incredibly real, it feels as if Sophie is really here. I can smell her, I can touch her, I can hear her.

My cock hardens in my hand, I can feel the heat creeping up my spine, she's going to make me come so hard and so damn fast. I feel like a horny teenager all over again.

"Mmm take it honey, suck it like a good girl. I'm going to come," Sophie grips my thighs hard and flicks her tongue across my tip, she reaches down to squeeze my balls and that's it. White hot pleasure hits me, lightning flashes behind my closed eyelids, heat rushes up my cock and I explode, shooting spurt after spurt of hot come down Sophie's throat as she swallows it all down.

"Ahh Sophie," I groan breathlessly.

I lie there for long minutes before I come back to earth and get my breathing under control and remember that I'm alone in my bed, I haven't come that hard in a very long time. I look down to see that I'm covered in come, it's on my abs, chest and even on my neck.

Shit, I'm in trouble.

The next few nights go the same way, waking in the middle of the night, taking my cock in my hand and losing myself to images of Sophie. Taking me in her mouth, sprawled out on my bed as I taste her, on her hands and knees whilst I pound into her from behind. I can't get enough of dream Sophie.

This is becoming a problem and now I have to face her at Trudie's for Lucie's birthday. I'm well and truly screwed.

# Chapter Twelve

## Sophie

It was early when I arrived at the café on Friday morning. Trudie has given me the whole day to work on Lucie's birthday cake ready for tomorrow. I have taken over one entire side of the kitchen where I have the mixers going, sugar shapes laid out on trays all ready to be assembled. It's now lunchtime and I'm just taking the cake out of the oven to cool when Trudie walks through the door.

"Ohhhh my it smells like heaven in here," she reaches for my face to brush off a speck of flour. I don't know why she bothered, I'm probably completely covered in it and I don't care one bit. I'm having the time of my life.

"How's it going in here?" she asks.

"Great, thanks for trusting me with this. I've not baked like this in such a long time".

"You're welcome Hun, you're a natural. You're wasted as a waitress. Oh my goodness that's it!" she exclaims.

"What's it?" I ask distractedly, whilst piping icing onto the cake, ready to put the two tiers together.

"You need to open a bakery!", she claps her hands excitedly.

"Oh no, I couldn't do that," I'm already shaking my head and talking myself down. Little does she know that I've always had this dream in my head to own a little bakery slash book shop, selling my own books of course. But that's all it is, a dream, something that I'd always wish for but I knew for a fact that it would never come true. I even know what I'd call it. 'Lost and Found', because even the most lost of souls can find themselves in the pages of a good book, with a yummy slice of cake of course.

"Hmm, we'll see about that," Trudie replies, it sounds more like a threat than a promise.

"Anyway, I came in here to let you know that Hugh is out in the café just dropping off party decorations for tomorrow. He's popping by early in the morning to get set up whilst Lucie is at her grandparents. He was asking after you," there's that mischievous smile on her face again.

"He was?" I ask, I can feel the blush creeping up my face. I haven't stopped thinking about that man since I met him, even more so since last Friday night when I felt and then saw his huge erection straining in his jeans. God I've had more than just a few saucy dreams about it this week and woken up with my hands down my pyjama shorts on multiple occasions. I still don't know what caused that reaction in him. It couldn't possibly have been me, could it?

"Yep!" Trudie says with a pop, pulling me out of my daydream.

"He was asking how the cakes going, shall I send him back so he can see for himself?". Oh God, I can't face him now can I, not after what I was just thinking about. But before I've even had a chance to answer her, she's turning and sashaying out of the swinging doors.

Oh no, oh no, oh no, I'm a total mess, he can't see my like this. I frantically wipe my hands on my apron and use a towel to try and wipe at the flour that I know is all over my face.

I sense him before I see him, the atmosphere in the room has changed. It's charged, as if someone has just plugged me into an electrical socket. My heart races, my pulse pounding, the blush is back and I'm still hiding behind my towel. I slowly lower it and see Hugh's epically handsome face smiling at me with an eyebrow raised.

"You hiding from me?", the deepness of his voice should be illegal. It's doing all sorts of things to my lady parts. He takes a few steps from the door and stops just in front of me, he reaches up and brushes his fingers lightly across my cheek. He then brings them to his lips and I swoon so hard, my knees almost buckle. I grip the table, desperately trying to save myself from becoming a giant horny heap on the floor.

"You had some icing ... on your cheek", his eyes are blazing. I can see my lust reflected back at me.

"Oh ... oh right. Thanks, so Trudie says you wanted to check on the cake?". I try to change the subject, I'm so wet my panties are completely ruined.

Hugh coughs and breaks the spell, "Not check up on. I know you're going to do a great job. The curiosity just got the better of me and I wanted to be nosy. If you don't mind of course?".

"Not at all, come and see". I lead him over to the work top and show him the two tiered red velvet cake I'd just put together. He moves along the work bench, looking closely at the edible flowers, leaves, blades of grass and butterflies I've made to decorate the cake with. The cake itself is going to be light pink, with a flower garden decorating the sides and butterflies perching on the top.

"Wow", Hugh says with awe in his voice. "You made these from scratch?", he asks, pointing to all the different shapes. I just nod at him and shrug my shoulders as if it's not a big deal. I spent my whole evening yesterday making all the sugar shapes from scratch, painting all the little details with edible paints. I was so focussed I didn't go to bed until well after midnight.

"Honey, these are amazing. I've never seen anything like it. Lucie is going to be blown away. It's going to be too good to eat".

Hugh's casual use of the nickname makes my heart flutter. I used to hate it when Liam called me 'babes', but Hugh calling me honey is given me all kinds of warm feelings.

"It's nowhere near finished yet, I need to finish icing the base and then put it all together. I've made a little topper with Lucie's name and age on it too. I guessed that she liked flowers and butterflies from the picture she made me a few weeks ago. That is right isn't it? Oh no, I should have checked with you first". I begin to panic, maybe I've made a mistake. Hugh's gentle hand falls onto my shoulder and he brings me to him in a hug, I can't help but notice how we fit together perfectly. I rest my cheek against his warm chest. I can feel his strong heart beat against my face, his heart is racing just like mine. He rubs small circles on my back and whispers in my ear "She's going to love the cake, butterflies and flowers are her favourite. She's been talking about you non stop since she met you so she's going to be more than excited that you've made it for her".

I don't have any words, I just nod. I haven't been held like this, maybe in forever. I always had to almost force Liam to show me any kind of physical affection but with Hugh it just feels so natural.

Hugh goes to step back, but before he does I feel a slight press against the top of my head and a small sigh sound from his chest. Did he just kiss me?

"Anyway, I'll let you get back to it. I'll see you tomorrow Soph". Hugh reaches for my hand and brings it to his mouth, pressing a small kiss to it before he turns and walks out of the kitchen before I can get my brain to function in order to form the words to say goodbye.

I managed to finish Lucie's cake just before closing. It's taken me the entire day but I'm pretty proud of it, hopefully she will love it, Hugh too.

Even though I'm exhausted I've gotten into the habit of heading over to the library after work most days. Life is starting to settle down, the sun is beginning to rise again and my mood has improved drastically since I arrived here almost two months ago. Sitting down with my laptop, a cup of coffee and my headphones on has become my therapy and the words have been flowing.

I've just sat down and gotten myself comfortable when Lily comes rushing over,

"Oh thank God you're here Sophie! I need to ask a massive favour".

"Hi Lily, of course, anything," *From the glint in her eye, I can tell I'm probably going to regret saying that.*

"So tomorrow is Lucie's birthday party at Trudie's, as you probably know of course. I heard you're making her birthday cake. Sorry I'm rambling, back to the point Lily!" she scolds herself. I can't help but laugh, she's usually so cool and calm. She's definitely flustered.

"So, anyway I was supposed to be doing a little storytelling thing at the party. Lucie is a massive bookworm so I planned to read the kids a story and then do some little activities afterwards. Elodie was supposed to be covering the library so I could be there. She's just called in ill, she has the flu and isn't going to be able to cover me tomorrow".

"Ok, well I'm sure Hugh will understand, it can't be helped when someone is unwell. I hope Elodie feels better soon".

"No ... Sophie you don't understand," she grips both of my hands in hers, imploring me to understand what she's trying to say.

"I can't let Lucie down, birthdays are a huge deal to Hugh. Lucie doesn't have her mum here obviously so Hugh always goes a little bit overboard, trying to make up for what she's missing". I can see the sadness in Lily's eyes, she really does think the world of Lucie, I still don't understand how I can help though.

"I get that, it must be hard on Hugh, I can't imagine the pressure he must feel," I tell Lily softly, I really can't imagine.

"Exactly," she states, "So I was kind of wondering if you're possibly free to do the book segment at the party? I checked with Trudie who already told me that you have the day off tomorrow, it'll only be for about an hour. I know Lucie would really love it", she smiles sweetly, begging me with her eyes.

"I'll owe you big time, I promise! You call in a favour in the future and I'm there, anything!".

"Oh Lils, I'm not sure ... they hardly know me, I wouldn't want to intrude. You're all so close. Plus, I have nothing prepared ..." I trail off.

"Well ... now don't get cross. I didn't mean to be nosy but you're in here everyday after work and I kind of, maybe a little bit, noticed some of your manuscripts next to you on the table". She smiles at me guiltily. "Soph, are you an author?" she asks.

So, here's the thing. I've never told anybody that I love to write, literally nobody, not even Liam. You would have thought being my partner and husband for such a long time that he maybe would have noticed but nope. I've never had the confidence to tell anybody, no other living human has ever heard my stories. I always read them to mum at her grave when I manage to visit but that doesn't count right?

I realise I still haven't answered Lily, whose staring at me, watching the inner war I'm having with myself. Am I ready to share my stories? Hmm, I'm not sure.

"I don't know Lily, I mean that was always the dream, I've been writing secretly for most of my adult life. Nobody has ever read any of my stories. What if they're no good?". I hate my own lack of confidence, I wish I was a little more like Maisie and was able to be just unapologetically me.

"Well, that's the other thing", she looks even more guilty this time.

"The other day when you left your stuff here when you went outside to take that phone call ... I maybe, just a little bit, by accident of course, read one of your stories. The one about the little bunny, it might be the sweetest story I've ever read".

I'm not sure if I should feel angry, upset, relieved, happy or if I should feel like she's violated my privacy, but the main thing I feel is curiosity.

"Wha.. what do you mean? You liked it?", I can't quite form words. Surely she's just saying that so I'll save her arse at the party tomorrow.

Lily grabs my hands again and sits down next to me,

"Soph it was beautiful. It was sweet, funny, adventurous and had a happy ending. Just what every story should have. You should be incredibly proud of yourself. I think the world needs to hear your stories babe".

"You think Lucie would like it?" I ask shyly.

"She would love it, bunnies are one of her favourite animals. She's been begging Hugh for one for the past six months!" that makes me smile. Could I share my stories, it'll only be to a bunch of kids right. They won't point and laugh and crush all my dreams will they? Screw it, this is my fresh start, this is my time to find myself and it's those thoughts that urge me to say ...

"Okaaaay?".

"That sounds more like a question babe, are you sure?", Lily laughs.

I think about it some more, "Yes, I'll do it".

Now to hurry home and spend my evening getting everything prepared! It's already been a busy day, it's about to get a lot busier.

## Chapter Thirteen

## Hugh

I awoke to squealing. Not upset squealing, not hurt squealing but bone deep excitement squealing. I can't help but smile to myself, I remember that feeling as a child when you'd wake up and remember it was your birthday or Christmas. Best feeling in the world. My parents have always made such a big deal of birthdays, even now as an adult, they always make sure birthdays are special and memorable.

Lucie is so lucky to have them in her life, and so am I. I couldn't imagine my life without my parents. Obviously I know that they won't be around one day and that brings a pain to my chest. We just have to make the most of our time together and appreciate every ounce of love they give.

Lucie comes bouncing into the bedroom and I barely have time to protect the crown jewels before she's jumping all over me in excitement. "It's my birthday Daddy! I four now, I almost a grown up just like you!".

"Steady on now Lulu, let's not get ahead of ourselves", I say with a chuckle. "Happy birthday my beautiful girl. You are my favourite person in the whole world". I kiss her forehead and pull her close to my chest. Lucie's birthdays have been hard since Gracie left us, this is our third birthday without her and I still miss her with every beat of my heart. But now is not the time to wallow. We have a party to get to.

"Right, up and at em'. Nana and Pop will be here soon to watch you while I get all your birthday surprises ready. But before that .... who would like some presents?!". And we are back to the squealing.

An hour later, I'm out of the door. Lucie had been so made up with her presents, especially the two baby bunnies that she'd been begging me for. She called them Honey and Pancake.

My truck is packed full of party supplies, it's bursting at the seams. Maybe I went a little overboard. I pull up outside Trudie's and Mitch is out of the door before I've even turned off the engine. He helps me with all the party supplies, bringing them into the café. I can't help but look around, searching for the gorgeous brunette who takes up way more space in my mind than I care to admit. She's not here, she made the cake of course but that doesn't mean she will be here today. Trudie already told me that she has the day off, although I can't help the pang of disappointment I feel in my chest.

No time to dwell though, we have a lot to do. The party starts in two hours so I better get to work.

Mitch and Trudie both help me to decorate the café, which includes rainbow balloons, banners, confetti, a balloon arch, dough-nut stand, photo props, party games, party poppers, you name it I've got it ... I may have gone too far this time. I'd do anything for that little girl though and I know she's going to love it all so much. I have all her favourites, including a craft station with a shit ton of glitter, obviously! Sweet table, mini disco with dance floor, loads of party games and a story time session with Lily to finish up with.

Trudie comes in through the kitchen doors with a flourish, she's wearing a bright yellow dress today ... I may need to grab my sunglasses out of my truck. My attention is quickly captured by the absolute masterpiece in her hands though. She is holding the most amazing cake I have ever seen in my life. I move in for a closer look, "Holy shit, would you look at that". The pink is Lucie's favourite shade, the butterflies perched on top look real, the grass blades and flowers look like they've been picked straight out of my garden. It's bloody fantastic!

"Didn't she do a good job?" Trudie states as she sets the cake on the buffet table. "That girl has such true talent, she's wasted here waiting tables".

"I might have to agree with you Trudie, that cake is the best cake I've ever seen in my entire life. It's too good to eat. We can't cut that right?". I look to Trudie for confirmation. She just laughs at me with raised eyebrows. "It's a cake Hugh, of course we have to cut it".

"Nope, not happening". I can't help the smirk on my face. Great, now I'm being overly protective over a damn cake.

I go back to setting out the plates and cups on the tables when the bell above the door rings, the atmosphere in the room shifts and there she is. Looking at me with a shy smile, God she's beautiful, I just want to kiss her. I cough and straighten, where did that come from? I'm married.

It takes a second to realise that Sophie is struggling through the door with her hands full of .... books, props, cushions, a blanket, craft supplies .... what's all that for? I hurry over to help,

"Hi... What's all this?"

"Erm well ... Lily wasn't able to leave the library. Elodie is unwell. She asked if ... well she asked if I could do the story time thing for her. I mean if that's ok with you? She didn't tell you?" She asks quietly with a frown, I could sense the worry radiating off of her.

"Of course it's fine. I'm sorry to put you out though, it's your day off. We can always just do something else".

"No! I mean it's fine. I'm happy to do it, I have everything prepared," she says with a smile. "Where do you want me?" *Spread out naked on my bed.*

Hmm inappropriate.

I show Sophie over to the section of the café where our favourite table is usually set up. Helping her to set down her boxes, I leave her to get set up. I can't help but keep peeking over at her though. She brought a lot of stuff with her. She's setting it all out carefully. When she bends to grab something else from the box I can't help but practically drool over her juicy peach of an arse. I just want to grab it and squeeze, massage down her legs and slide my fingers into her panties to see how wet she is. Wow you would think that all the jerking off I've been doing would have taken the wind out of my sails but no, my dick is so hard it's trying to break out of my jeans.

A throat clears, and I look up at Trudie's smirking face. Damn it, busted. "She sure is a beauty isn't she?" Trudie rests a hand on my arm and nods towards where Sophie is now sitting cross legged on a rainbow cushion, setting out books, colouring pages, crayons and little rainbow tote bags.

"She really is", my voice trails off.

She's the most gorgeous woman I've ever laid eyes on. It's not just how she looks though, it's her. She's sweet, she comes across really shy but I could tell that she has a kind heart. When she told me about all the shit her husband has put her through, I wish I could meet him just so I could punch him in the face on her behalf. How do you have an absolutely stunning, kind, beautiful, gentle soul like Sophie as your wife. Yet turn your back on her just to get your rocks off with someone else. It truly is a mystery to me. Why is it that the worst things always happen to the best people.

Before I know it, the party is in full swing. Lucie's face when she walked in was an absolute picture. She came bounding through the door, shouted "Ding!" and then stood frozen, slack jawed for a good twenty seconds before the squealing started up again. We all burst into laughter, I swear that kid is going to be an actress or something equally drama filled when she grows up. The sass is out of this world.

So I'm currently sat on a mini chair, my arse almost touching the floor and my knees almost touching my ears. I mean I'm a huge 6'3 man, whose managed to squeeze himself onto a tiny chair whilst covered head to toe in glitter. I'm going to be finding this stuff for weeks.

It must be a sight to behold because every time I look up, I meet the beautiful green eyes of Sophie already watching me, with laughter in her eyes. I motion to her to come and join me, I've been abandoned by the four year olds now anyway as they spin around the dance floor. She comes and sits next to me, somehow looking much more comfortable on the tiny chair than I do. "Well, don't you look beautiful," she giggles, pointing at the glitter which is just about everywhere.

"I have no idea what you mean, I'm the prettiest princess in the room ... almost".

"Hmm almost, who beats you then?", she looks so pretty when she smiles.

"Well obviously Lucie ... and you too". With that I lift my glitter filled hand above her head and unleash it with a laugh. It drifts from my hand and flutters down covering her hair, cheeks, lips and settles across the delectable bumps of her breasts. She looks at me with her mouth gaping open for all of three seconds before she grabs a pot of glitter from the table and dumps the entire thing on my head. Her eyes wide, hands covering her sweet mouth as she belly laughs uncontrollably. I've never heard her laugh like that, it makes my chest ache.

Before she can fathom what's happening, I haul her out of her chair and start chasing her around the table. We throw handfuls of glitter at each other, all the kids join in, howling with laughter. I've not had this much fun in ... well ever.

The kids eventually all disappear back over to the dance floor, taking a ton of glitter with them. I'm going to have to get this place professionally cleaned for Trudie, for sure.

I somehow manage to crowd Sophie into the corner of the café, both hands full of glitter. She backs away from me laughing, a huge smile plastered across her face, until her back presses against the wall. I keep moving closer and closer until our chests are pressed together, her head is arched back to look into my eyes. Everybody else's attention is firmly on the kids, we are hidden behind one of Trudie's giant house plants.

I don't know what's come over me but I press harder, I can feel her breath on my neck and I can see her pulse fluttering in hers. I move my hands to her face and leave behind two bright pink glitter prints. Her eyes flick to my lips and back to my eyes. My heart is pounding in my chest, the room and everyone else has fizzled out around us. It's just me and Sophie. Hidden together in the corner of the room and she's looking up at me with those gorgeous fuck me eyes. There is something magnetic about this woman, she calls to some place deep inside of my soul. I'd managed to go almost three years not feeling an ounce of attraction for a woman, but one glance at this one and I was ready to throw all caution to the wind and say 'What the hell?' and go for it anyway.

Her soft pink lips are open and waiting, they look so inviting I want to devour her. Time stands still, I can hear my heart beat thumping in my ears. Sophie lets out a small moan and closes her eyes, that's when I realise that I'm pressed so tightly against her, my hard cock is pressed right up against the seam of her jeans. I press forward harder and she almost purrs.

She wants me just as much as I want her, her chest is moving up and down fast, causing her breasts to bounce with every breath. I want to strip her naked and suck on her nipples as she writhes beneath me. We stay frozen, pushed together tightly, time stands still as I subtly grind my hardness against her and stare into her eyes. I could come just like this, dry humping her like a horny teenager.

"Daddy," Lucie comes bounding around the plant and plasters herself against the back of my legs. Sophie and I break apart, both breathing heavily, still staring into each others eyes in disbelief. That's when I remember where I am. Holy shit, I'm at my kids birthday party in a packed café, with all our friends and family and I'm hiding in the corner dry humping the fuck out of the new waitress. What the fuck. I rub my hands down my face, which only spreads the pink glitter further. Looking back at Sophie, she smiles before placing a hand on my lower arm and leaning forward to whisper in my ear "It's ok". And walks away, swaying that fine arse as she goes.

I can feel eyes on me, and look around to find Ace staring at me. The bastard just winks at me with a smirk on his face and goes back to his conversation, having seen the entire thing.

But it's not ok is it, it's not just the giant rod of steel trying to break a hole through my jeans that's the problem. It's the fact that she makes my heart flutter and ache in ways I promised myself I wouldn't feel for anybody but my wife.

An hour later and I'm sat in awe, much like everybody else around me. The party had been a hit, everyone had been having a great time and the kids were exhausted. Things were wrapping up and the kids were sat listening to Sophie's story time session.

I was just as mesmerised as the kids. Not only was the story really cute and well written but it was her voice, the emotion she put into her words as if she had written them herself. She spoke softly, giving each child eye contact and when she briefly met my eyes it was as if she was peering deep into my soul.

She had made each child a little story pack with a printed copy of the book, colouring sheets, crayons, a little bunny mask and some sweets, all put together in a little rainbow tote bag. How she managed to pull this altogether so quickly was beyond me.

Movement pushed up against my arm and I looked down at Lily with a smile on her face. She wrapped her hands around my bicep and pressed her cheek against me, "Amazing isn't she?".

"Mesmerising", I couldn't take my eyes off of Sophie.

"Hold up, you're not supposed to be here. How are you here?" I asked Lily.

"Oh, I saw an opportunity to give someone special a confidence boost and I went for it. I'm sorry I missed most of the party but this was important".

"What do you mean?" I took Lily by the hand and pulled her to the back of the café where we could whisper without disturbing the story. All eyes were on Sophie so nobody even noticed that we had crept back.

"Sophie works everyday here at the café and every evening she comes to the library, laptop in hand and a giant bag of papers which she hauls around with her. She writes for hours and hours, everyday. Lost in her own little world, she's been at it for weeks. Last week, Sophie got a phone call while she was there and went outside to take it, I couldn't help but have a little snoopy snoop," she looked up at me, waiting for me to say something. All I could do was nod to encourage her to continue her story.

"She has an entire bag of manuscripts Hughie ... children's stories, romance novels, notebooks full of writing. She came back in from her phone call looking super stressed so I didn't say anything at the time. But yesterday, I saw an opportunity and I took it. She's hiding all this amazing writing, I just gave her a little push to share something".

Lily looked sad for Sophie, I think we had all picked up on the fact that she was hurting, it was nice that she'd found a friend.

"Are you telling me that Sophie wrote this story?", I couldn't believe my ears. I had no idea. You could tell the story was a total hit by the silence in the room, a group of four year old kids were sat in awe of her.

"Yep, this is the story I read that day in the library. She's talented isn't she?".

"It's amazing Lily, I had no idea". Awe echoing in my voice.

"I think there's a lot that we don't know about her Hughie, she's hurting right now, she's been through a huge trauma. That bastard of a husband hurt her in ways I can't even begin to imagine. She fits in here, she's growing here. I think we are going to see who she truly is soon enough". Lily patted my arm and walked away to find Ace and I think I'd subconsciously decided there and then that I was going to get to the bottom of who Sophie really is and who she's meant to be.

# Chapter Fourteen

## Sophie

It had been two months since I'd left Liam, two months ago my entire life imploded and I lost everything and two months since I moved here to Meadowside and began making a new life for myself.

I had a job which I enjoyed, working with two people who cared for me as if I were their family. I'd started making friends, true friends who cared about me. Initially I'd been upset that Lily had snooped through my things but I could see the bigger picture. She was curious, I knew she meant well and she seemed to have the biggest heart, she was turning out to be a really special friend. I could feel myself getting stronger, I was starting to feel less weighed down by everything that had happened to me and I knew that I was going to be alright.

That's what gave me the confidence and strength to file for divorce last week. I had known since the minute I'd left Liam that I wouldn't be going back and he hadn't even tried to follow me and win me back. It was over and I was now ready for it to be official. I was sad that my marriage was ending, Liam had been the only man I'd ever loved but I believed that everything happened for a reason and maybe it just wasn't meant to be. He had never given me butterflies, made my hairs stand up on end and tingle, blimey he'd never even given me an orgasm. *He'd never made me feel like Hugh does.* I'd been saving my wages from Trudie's and I still had some of my inheritance from when my parents passed so I got in touch with my lawyer who drew up divorce papers. They were delivered to Liam two days later and that's when the phone calls began. He was relentlessly phoning and texting me, none of which I answered. I had said everything I'd needed to say that day when I left.

It was Monday evening and I'd just gotten home from my evening at the library when my phone buzzed yet again, I didn't even need to check the caller I.D, I knew it was him. The buzzing stopped and a few seconds later a text came through ...

> **Liam: Babe, please answer the phone. I need to talk to you. I think I've made a huge mistake. L x**

Ha, you think? How dare he, he's put me through hell and now he realises he's made a mistake. What a surprise. Another text comes through seconds later ...

> **Liam: Tell me where you are, I can come down and we can have a chat. See if we can sort this mess out together. L x**

Yep, that wasn't going to happen. I was finally learning to like who I was without Liam. Reading my story at Lucie's birthday party had been a huge confidence boost for me. A group of people, children and adults, had sat in silence and listened to me read. When I'd finished, the hooting and hollering was so loud I had been completely stunned. I had received so many hugs, comments and compliments, many of them asking what the hell I was doing working as a waitress. By the time I'd fought my way through the crowd, I realised that there was only one persons opinion I wanted to hear. *Hugh's.*

He had immediately pulled me into a hug and told me how amazing I was, that he was proud of me and that he thought I could really do something special with my writing. I had felt more seen in that moment than I had in the last fifteen years of my life with Liam. He hadn't even known that I'd been writing until the day he saw me packing up my belongings.

Another text came through, was he not getting the hint that I had no intention of replying to him ...

> **Liam: I am your husband and I have every right to know where you are. I still have access to your bank accounts and phone records, I can find you if you don't tell me yourself Soph. Don't make me come looking for you. L x**

Bit late for that isn't it, pulling the 'I'm your husband' card. And why did that last message sound like a threat. Liam had never threatened me, he'd never raised his voice, he was almost entirely indifferent to me. I wasn't sure which was worse. I was well aware of the fact that Liam's baby would have been born by now, why was he messaging me? Should he not be worrying about his new woman and child?

I didn't care any more, I switched my phone off and went to take a bath.

The next few weeks flew by, I spent my time working at the café, evenings at the library and weekends with my new friends. The girls had invited me to lunch, coffee and out for drinks again at Jax's. I'd never felt more like I belonged than I did at this moment.

I'd also spent time with Hugh, he invited me to join him and Lucie for coffee when they came to visit on a Saturday. Trudie encouraged it, still with that mischievous look in her eye. It was nice spending time with them both, getting to know them. Hugh was an amazing Dad and you could see how much he doted on Lucie.

As for Lucie, she is probably the cutest kid I've ever met. She has the most adorable big brown eyes, which she definitely uses to wrap everybody around her little finger.

I was enjoying my time here, it was beginning to feel like home. Of course, I still heard from Liam every single day. He still hadn't signed the divorce papers which was beginning to weigh me down. I'd spoken to my lawyer about it and he said that all we can really do is wait him out. He felt strongly that one day we would get the outcome we wanted. I wasn't so sure, for some reason Liam wasn't playing ball. You would have thought that having a new family would make him want to get things sorted sooner rather than later, but for some reason he was making things difficult. He had never fought for me a day in his life, why did he care so much now?

It was now early December and I'd decided it was time to get festive. Christmas had always been my favourite time of year when my parents were still alive. My mum would always make the holidays extra special. Not just with gifts but with everything, she would make the most delicious food and we would spend hours together playing board games, watching movies and just being together. They are some of my most magical memories and I hope that one day I get to recreate it all with a family of my own. Christmas was a feeling, not just a time to spoil each other with gifts. It was a time for love. I long for it, I long to have a love like my parents. They were married for 42 years and they died within a matter of weeks of each other. We lost Dad first ... then Mum died three weeks later, of a broken heart I'm sure.

Freya had told me about a lovely little Christmas tree farm a few miles down the road so I climbed into my car and off I went. It was the first weekend of December and I could see people putting up their decorations and carrying their trees inside as I drove the quiet streets.

When I pulled into 'Festive Franks Tree Farm', memories of my childhood hit me. It was absolutely jam packed full of trees of all shapes and sizes. Twinkly lights were draped around some of the biggest trees in the entrance and it was just starting to get dark, getting close to closing. I'd purposely come late in the day to avoid the busy crowds.

There was a huge archway to walk through to get onto the farm, it was decorated beautifully with flowers, lights, pine cones and little red bows. There was a little hot chocolate shack with hay bales to sit on while you drank. Everybody was wrapped up tight in their winter warmers. This place was happiness wrapped up in a bow.

I was in absolutely no hurry to choose a tree and leave, so I got myself a hot chocolate with marshmallows and whipped cream and wandered up and down the aisles of trees. The smell was absolutely amazing. I couldn't help but reach out and brush the pines as I walked past, breathing in that fresh pine scent.

"Sophie! Sophie over here!", looks like I wasn't the only one on the hunt for their Christmas tree this weekend. Walking down the aisle towards me were Maisie and Mack, Freya and Ryan, Lily and Ace, and trailing behind were Hugh and Lucie. My heart skipped a beat in my chest.

Lucie saw me and ran past everybody and straight into my arms, "Sophie, you here. We come to get a Christmas tree, You come to get a tree too?". She warmed my heart, we had grown quite close over the past few weeks and it brought a huge smile to my face that she was so excited to see me.

"I am here to buy a tree, aren't they all so beautiful? I'm finding it so hard to pick one".

"We are going to get the biggest one! It's going to touch the roof! Aren't we Daddy?" Lucie looked to Hugh who was stood watching with a curious smile. Our eyes met, I could see the flicker of heat in his. It was definitely reflected in my own.

"Well Lulu, I'm not sure we will fit a tree that big into our little cottage but we are sure going to try. Uncle Mack might have to get his chainsaw out to help us make it fit".

"Uncle Mack always makes it fit", Maisie muttered under her breath just loud enough for us adults to hear. Hugh barked out a laugh and Mack buried his head in his hands with a chuckle, "No comment".

"Well .... anyway, do you need some help picking a tree and getting it attached on the roof?" Hugh turned to me. He was so sweet and helpful.

"That would be so helpful, thank you. I didn't quite think that far ahead before I came. I was just going to ask a worker to help me out. But if you're sure it's no trouble?".

"Of course not, happy to help honey". There goes my heart fluttering again. It was going to flutter right out of my chest one of these days. Hugh and I had gotten to know each other better over the weeks and the fluttering in my heart was only getting stronger. Fluttering was happening in other places too but that was for thinking about later.

"Hey, why don't we all take Lucie Lu here for some hot chocolate and cookies while you help Sophie?", Ace asked Hugh.

"Yes Daddy! I want chocolate with Uncle Ace!".

"Sounds good to me kiddo, I'll come and find you guys when we're done". Ace took Lucie by one hand, Lily took the other and the seven of them headed off through the farm to the hot chocolate shack.

"She's so lucky to have so many amazing people who love her so much", I looked up a Hugh as he watched Lucie go.

"She is, we both are. Those guys are our family. Come on then, lead the way, let's go and find you a tree".

We walked up and down the aisles, making small talk, in no hurry at all. I could feel his eyes on me, warming me from head to toe. I was pretty certain he was staring at my arse. Every time Hugh reached to touch a tree his fingers brushed against mine and tingles shot up my arm. He was standing so close to me that I could smell him, the mix of man, soap and pine was heady. His warmth pressed against my back as he reached to touch the branches.

"How about this one?" his voice echoed in my ear, I could feel his warm breath on my neck. His hard chest pushed against my back. I couldn't take a full breath let alone answer him. We both stood silently, my back to his chest, both breathing hard. His big hands wrapped around my hips and he pushed against me harder, as though he just couldn't hold back.

"Honey, what are you doing to me?", he said in a breathy whisper.

"The same thing you're doing to me", I didn't even recognise my own voice. I could feel his rock solid erection pressed against my back, he was still holding me tight. I couldn't stop myself from pushing against him, he groaned in my ear and held my hips hard enough to leave small bruises. I didn't care, I wanted him to mark me so I could relive this moment later when I was alone.

Hugh slowly pushed me forward by the hips, keeping his pushed tightly to mine. We slowly walked forward until we were behind the tree when Hugh whipped me around. He moved his hands to my face and held me close, we were nose to nose. His warm breath caressing my face. He looked from my eyes to my lips and back again. A moment of uncertainty flashed in his eyes, it was gone a second later.

"Fuck it," he whispered and slammed his lips to mine. I clung to the lapels of his jacket and pulled him closer. His lips were soft, his breath minty. The kiss started off slow, caressing each others lips until I felt the soft swipe of his tongue and I opened up for him. Our tongues tangled together, caressing and licking. I couldn't get him close enough, I wanted to climb this man like a tree.

As if he had heard my thoughts, he brushed his hands down my back, to my arse. He grabbed me and hauled me up, wrapping my legs around his tight waist. He leaned me up against the wall next to the tree. I could feel his hardness as he ground his hips into me. He was rock solid ... and huge. He held me up against him, our lips and tongues devouring each other, I'd never felt this pure electricity and passion in my life. In this moment, this man could do whatever he wanted to me, I wouldn't stop him.

Hugh pulled back to look into my eyes, whatever he saw in them had him coming back for more. His cock was a steel rod, pushed perfectly against the seam of my jeans. I held tightly onto his shoulders for leverage and began to grind my pussy against his crotch. He used his hands on my arse to control the speed and pressure as I climbed higher. My pussy was warm and wet, I was going to come if we didn't stop.

"Don't stop", Hugh whimpered against my cheek. I couldn't stop even if I tried. I rode him, fully clothed. Our breaths mingled together, our chests heaving, I was hot. Hugh had sweat beading on his forehead as he whipped his winter hat off and threw it to the ground. We ground against each other hard for long minutes, whispering soft words in each others ears, in between kisses.

The warmth crept up my spine and I was seconds from exploding, "Hugh, I ... I think I'm gonna come". We were full on fucking now with our clothes on. His fingers were bruising my arse cheeks as I ground against him like my life depended on it. He kissed me once more and bit my lip and that was it.

Warmth flooded through me as my orgasm took hold, white flashes sparked behind my eyelids as I came apart in his arms. I felt like I'd gone deaf and blind, all I could feel was the buzzing in my body. I continued to ride him through it and before I could fathom what was happening, Hugh gently put me down on my feet, scrambled to undo his belt and pulled his jeans and briefs just below his arse, he took his hard cock in one hand, which was even bigger now that it was free.

He pulled me close with the other hand as he groaned in my ear. He moved his hand up and down his hard length, once, twice. Slammed his lips to mine as he came apart all over the ground below us. I held him close, peppering kisses up and down his jaw as he came all over his hand with a groan, "Ohhh honey". This was the single hottest moment of my entire existence, I didn't even care that we were in public and could get caught at any second.

He held me close for long seconds as he came back down to earth, his eyes were closed, his chest heaving, he was still and quiet. He gave me one last lingering kiss on my lips before he stepped back. "Fuck," he said with an embarrassed chuckle.

I reached into my coat pocket and pulled out a travel size pack of tissues and offered them to him with a shy smile. "Thank you honey". After Hugh cleaned himself up and tucked himself back into his jeans, he reached for me and held me close. "I ... I didn't mean for that to happen, I'm sorry. Was that ok?". God he was so thoughtful and kind.

"Hugh," I took his face in my hands and looked into this beautiful man's big blue eyes "That was beyond ok, unexpected, but extremely hot. But, what does this mean? What happens now? I don't want things to be awkward between us, I really like you Hugh. You're a special man but things are tricky, I'm going through a divorce and you have a busy life with Lucie ...." I trailed off, not wanting to mention the whole situation with him being a widower.

He pulled my hands from his face and held them in his, he looked so uncertain in this moment I couldn't help but hold my breath and brace for impact.

"I like you too honey. I mean, if it wasn't totally obvious. You know", he shrugged and laughed as he gestured down to the come covering the ground beneath us. He looked down at his feet, took a deep breath before he looked back into my eyes.

"I haven't been with anybody since Grace died almost three years ago. I never thought I'd ever be able to move on and have anything with anybody else. My priority since then has been Lucie, everything I do is for Lucie. I never saw myself moving on or ever feeling anything for another woman". He fell silent and my heart broke just a little. This was stupid, what was I doing. I wasn't even divorced yet and I was humping a man to orgasm in the middle of a Christmas tree farm. Not just any man, but a heart broken single dad who had lost his wife.

I took a step back to give us some space, "I get it Hugh. I understand. I'm sorry". I forced a small smile, one that I didn't feel. I felt embarrassed and foolish, how could I possibly have feelings for someone after all I'd been through recently. I was being naïve and living in a fantasy.

"No Sophie, that's not what I meant". Hugh stepped closer and slipped his hands around my waist, pulling me closer to him. He rested his lips against my forehead. I couldn't see his face but I could feel his heart pounding against my hands. "I like you, like you. Since the moment I saw you at Trudie's that day I've thought you were the most beautiful woman I'd ever seen, I can't get you out of my head. I fought it because I felt like it was wrong. My wife may not be here with us any more but I felt like I'd be betraying her if I was to pursue anything with you".

"I know, and I understand. I can't imagine being in your position and I truly accept how you feel and will accept however you want to move forward". I snuggled into his chest, feeling like this may be the most short lived romance in history. I soaked in his warmth, just in case this was my last chance.

We stood in silence for a long while, wrapped in each others arms before Hugh spoke, "I'd like to try honey. I owe it to myself, Lucie and you to give this a try and see where it goes. It may not be easy and I don't know how I'll handle a lot of things. This is all new for me, the trying to move on thing. I made a promise to my wife before she died, I promised I'd try to live my life and move on. I didn't mean it at the time, but I feel it now, with you. You're a special lady Sophie and you make me feel things that I haven't felt in a long time. So if you're willing to give me a chance and can have some patience with me, I'd like to see where this goes. I'd like to take you on a date". He looked at me with uncertainty, pain, longing and a little dash of hope in his eyes.

"I'd like that too". I whispered as I lowered my face into his neck.

We found a tree, ironically it was the one we'd just rubbed each other to orgasm against, secured it to my car roof, exchanged phone numbers and said our goodbyes with plans to go to dinner later on in the week.

Well, that wasn't the festive outing I had been expecting, it was so much more than I could have ever wished for and the heart fluttering was at an all time high. Could I really be considering the possibility of a new relationship so soon after the breakdown of my marriage? I think I just might be.

# Chapter Fifteen

**Hugh**

*Dear Sweetheart,*
*It's three weeks until Christmas, your favourite time of year.*
*Lucie is growing so fast, I just know that this Christmas is*
*going to be a magical one. We went and got our Christmas tree*
*at the weekend, a huge seven footer! Lucie's choice of course,*
*we had to get Mack round to chop the trunk a little so it didn't*
*touch the ceiling!*
*Lucie loved it though, we decorated it with lights and all*
*of our ornaments. We ate cookies, sang Christmas songs*
*and watched Christmas movies too, just like you'd always*
*dreamed of doing with her.*
*You're always here with us Grace, no matter what. You are*
*always in our hearts, you will always be a part of us, both of*
*us. You know that don't you? You'll never be forgotten.*
*So, here's the thing, I asked Sophie out on a date. My first date*
*since I lost you almost three years ago. I'm excited, nervous,*

> *scared... hurting too if I'm totally honest, but I'm also feeling kind of hopeful.*
> *But I just wanted to, no, needed to tell you that I'll always love you, you'll always be in my heart, no matter what and I hope you're happy wherever you are.*
> *Love Always,*
> *Hugh x*

I'd just finished work and picked Lucie up from pre-school, she was sitting in the back of the car chattering away, telling me all about her day. I loved hearing the happiness and excitement in her voice.

We were on our way to the cemetery to visit Grace before we went home for dinner. Lucie has spent the last week busy creating pictures and writing little notes for Grace. Her little writing is so cute, all her letters back to front but they meant a lot to her and she knew exactly what she was trying to say.

We came to visit Grace every week and always brought our pictures and letters along with us. When Grace died and we had her funeral, Mack had made a gorgeous wooden waterproof letterbox for us to keep at Grace's grave, we always brought along our letters and posted them so that Grace could keep them close.

Only Grace knows whether she sees them, but it brings me comfort to know that I'm doing my best to keep her involved. I write most weeks, it's something what makes me feel close to her. It brings me peace. I'm not sure if I'll ever be ready to stop writing so much.

We pulled up into the car park, grabbed our letters and the daisies we bought every week. As we headed up the path to the grave, I spotted a woman sat in front of Grace's headstone. I could tell from here that it was Freya. Freya and Grace had been incredibly close sisters before Grace died, I know that it hurt

Freya tremendously that her sister wasn't here any more. They were only three years apart, Freya being the eldest.

As we got closer, I could see Freya's shoulders moving up and down softly. She was crying and it broke my heart. Freya and I had always been close, she felt like my very own sister. I set Lucie on a nearby bench, gave her my phone to watch a video.

"Can you be a super big girl for me and stay here for a little bit, Auntie Fifi is feeling a bit sad and Daddy's going to go and see if she's ok".

"Ok Daddy, I hug her too in a minute". My girl had the biggest heart and the understanding and compassion of a child twice her age.

I approached Freya, loud enough for her to hear me coming. I rested my hand on her shoulder as she turned her tear stained eyes up to me.

"Oh Fifi, come here". She threw herself into my arms, sobbing into my chest, "I just miss her so much Hughie, she's meant to be here with us".

"I know Freya, I know. I miss her too". I held her close, Freya looks so much like Grace. They were always mistaken for twins growing up.

We held each other for a long time, not saying anything, I tried hard to blink back the tears in my own eyes but a few snuck free. Freya reached up to wipe them away with her thumbs.

"Will it ever get any easier Hughie?" Freya asked softly.

"Hmm, I don't think it'll ever get easier but we will learn to live with the pain. It'll become manageable. The best thing we can do is to keep living, Grace wouldn't want us to be sad. She wanted us to carry on living, for her. Do everything you dream of doing Freya, don't hold back. Laugh, cry, have fun, get married, have babies, do it all. Grace is always with us, she may not be here for us to hold but she lives on in our hearts".

That's the thing about losing someone you love, the pain will never go away, it'll never lessen and you'll never miss them any less. You just manage to live with it, for yourself and for others.

I'd like to believe that we will all be back together again one day. I hold onto the hope that Grace is here with us, I still feel her all around me. I know she loves us and we will always love her.

"Hughie ... when did you get so wise big guy?" Freya laughed, whilst wiping away the last of her tears. I didn't even have to think about it, I answered with no hesitation,

"You see that little girl over there?" I pointed towards Lucie, who was currently sat belly laughing so loudly at something on my phone.

"That little girl has taught me the meaning of life, the meaning of love. It doesn't matter what material things we have, it doesn't matter how much money we have. What matters is that we have our loved ones, even when they aren't physically here with us any more, they're always here with us in our hearts. Everything I do is for that little girl, I want to show her more love and happiness than she could ever imagine. But it's important not to shield her from the sad times too, as that's when we learn and grow". I reached out and took Freya's hand.

"We'll be alright Fifi, she's here with us. She lives on in that little girl". Lucie looked up at us both, laughter tears in her eyes. Her video must have finished as she hopped off the bench and ran into Freya's arms, she reached her tiny little hands up and rested them on Freya's cheeks, leaning forward to kiss the end of her nose "Don't be sad Auntie Fifi, Mummy loves you".

And that set us off crying again, this time happy tears.

# Chapter Sixteen

## Sophie

Liam: Where are you?

Liam: Please answer me.

Liam: I need to know you're ok.

Liam: Come on Soph, it's me, your husband. I need you to tell me where you are.

> **Liam: I miss you, you've been gone for so long. When are you coming home?**

> **Liam: Sophie, if you don't reply to me I will come looking for you! What's going on? Are you fucking someone else? I will find you.**

> **Me: Liam. Please stop texting me. I'm not coming home, ever. You are the only person at fault here, not me. Go back to your new woman and baby. We are over.**

It was time. I'd finally made a decision that I should have made years ago. For years Liam and I tried to have children, well I tried, Liam barely gave me the 'attention' required for making a baby. While the reasons behind that are obvious now, they definitely hadn't been then.

I've held onto a fear that I'm unable to have children, the thought of that truly breaks my heart . I was meant to be a mother, I know it deep in my bones. Living with the what ifs were driving me crazy and it was time to know once and for all what was going on inside this body of mine.

I'd made an appointment with the GP to get things rolling. As I'm waiting in the waiting room my heart is pounding in my chest, my hands are sweaty, I feel nauseous. But I couldn't hide from this any more, I needed to know.

As my name was called I carried myself on shaky legs into the consultation room and told the nice doctor my story.

"Well, it definitely sounds like something we should perhaps look into. Being that you are only thirty two you are still in the prime window for pregnancy. I'd like to take some blood work and send that off for testing, if that's ok with you Mrs Taylor?".

I agreed to whatever testing was available, had my height and weight measurements taken, blood pressure checked and answered countless questions about my general health and well-being.

As the conversation was wrapping up the doctor asked if I'd been using any contraception within the last few years.

"No, nothing at all. We decided around four years ago that we were going to try for a baby. Before that I was on the pill. It took a few months for my period to straighten itself out but since then we haven't taken any precautions at all".

"Thank you Mrs Taylor, I think that's everything for now. Your blood test results should be back within a few days. How about we make another appointment for the end of the week, for us to discuss the results. As we are getting closer to Christmas, I'd like to get a plan in place before the break".

We spoke a little more, with plans made for me to come back on the Friday for my blood test results. I was apprehensive but relieved that I'd taken the steps to figure out my future.

But before then I have my very first date with Hugh to look forward to tomorrow night. We were driving a little out of town to go to a steakhouse for dinner. I couldn't wait. It had been a very long time since I'd been on a date, let alone a first date. Liam and I skipped all of that, we were pretty much children when we met. And when we were married I barely saw him, let alone go on a date with him.

I had the afternoon off work so decided to go and find myself a nice dress for my date. I also had a hair and nail appointment. I never really made much effort before, I'd always felt a bit frumpy if I'm honest. I'd lost a lot of my self confidence over the years.

I suppose that's what happens when your husband doesn't make you feel sexy or desired.

Hours later when I got home I felt amazing! I'd had a new haircut and some subtle highlights put in. My nails were a pretty pink and I felt shiny and brand new. I was just about to get in the bath when my phone dinged with a text, I couldn't help but roll my eyes. Liam had been relentless, texting multiple times every single day, swinging between begging me to go home and making out that I was out whoring it up and that the breakdown of our marriage was my fault. So obviously the divorce papers were still unsigned and I was still waiting. I picked up my phone with a sigh, here we go. Much to my surprise the text message wasn't from Liam. It was from Hugh, which sent warm flutters to my tummy and a smile to my face.

> **Hugh: Hey honey. How was your day? I'm really looking forward to our date on Thursday. H x**

> **Me: Hi Hugh. I'm good thanks. I had a doctor's check-up this afternoon, then went and got my hair and nails done. I feel brand new. I'm looking forward to Thursday too. How're you doing? S x**

> **Hugh: I'm so glad you had some time for yourself today, I already know you look beautiful. You always do. I'm good thanks honey, I took Lucie to see Grace**

today after work. Freya was there and she was upset. We took her for hot chocolate and cake to cheer her up. We missed you while we were at Trudie's. H x

Me: I'm sorry to hear that Freya was sad, I'll get in touch with her. See if we can have a girls' night. She's been a good friend to me since I got here. S x

Hugh: I'd appreciate that and I know Freya will too. She's lucky to have you, as am I. Anyway duty calls, I have a little girl shouting at me about rubber ducks! I'll swing by and pick you up at 7 pm on Thursday beautiful, Goodnight. H x

Me: Goodnight Hugh. See you soon. Give Lucie a hug from me. S x

God that man gives me the warm and fuzzies. Just as I drop myself into the bath another text comes through. Hugh must have forgotten to say something.

Liam: You better not be seeing someone else Sophie. You are MY WIFE.

And just like that, my warm and fuzzies disappear.

# Chapter Seventeen

## Hugh

I was nervous, beyond nervous. I hadn't been on a date in a very long time. The last date I went on was with my wife, the week before we received her cancer diagnosis.

I'd made myself a promise tonight though, I wasn't going to think about the past, I wasn't going to wallow in guilt and uncertainty, I was going to live. For Grace, for myself, for Lucie and for Sophie.

I'd never met anybody quite like Sophie, she was petite, quiet, shy and so damn beautiful. But I could tell that she had a fire in her eyes, a determination. I wasn't quite sure what it was for yet but I sure was going to have fun getting to know her better and find out.

It was 7pm on the dot as I stood on Sophie's doorstep ready to knock, I'd been sat outside in my truck for the past ten minutes trying to work up the courage.

Before I had a chance to knock on the door though, it swung open and there she was. I was momentarily stunned.

"Holy shit", I muttered. Sophie was wearing a gorgeous skin tight navy blue body con dress which stopped just above her knees, a knee length white coat and matching navy heels. Her legs were smooth and tanned and went on for days. I slowly swept my eyes back up her body, her curves were so sinful I couldn't help but bring my fist up to my mouth and bite down on a groan.

Up and up my eyes went, her hair was loose in big chocolate curls down her back. Her make up was mostly natural with gorgeous pink lipstick. I couldn't help but imagine what that pink would look like around the base of my cock. My dick twitched in my jeans.

When I finally looked her in the eye, she was looking at me with amusement, "Like what you see?" she asked shyly.

"Oh fuck yeah, honey you are absolutely stunning". I watched the blush spread from her chest up to her cheeks, she really was beautiful.

"You don't look so bad yourself handsome", she rested a hand on my chest and went up on her toes to press a light kiss to my cheek. I couldn't help myself as I brought my hands around her waist and pulled her closer for a proper kiss.

"Get that lipstick all over me honey". My voice was husky and deep and I didn't miss her full body shiver when I pulled her against me. The kiss started off light and innocent, but quickly turned frantic as we battled for power. I slid my tongue into her mouth, my heart was frantically beating in my chest, my cock was hard, if we didn't get out of here soon I was going to take her inside and bend her over the back of her sofa. It had been way too long since I'd had sex, my will to hold back was hanging on by a thread.

I reluctantly pulled back "Come on beautiful, or we'll never make it to dinner". Both of our chests were heaving as I took her by the hand and led her down to my truck, I helped her climb inside before I made my way around the car and got inside to drive. As soon as I closed the door her scent enveloped me, fresh raspberries and vanilla, I'd never forget that smell.

It was a relatively quick drive to the restaurant, we made small talk in the car. Sophie told me all about her week at work and we spoke lots about Lucie. Before we knew it we had arrived and I helped Sophie out of the car and led her into the restaurant with my hand pressed to the bottom of her back.

We both ordered sirloin steak with creamy potatoes au gratin and sautéed asparagus, it was absolutely delicious. We enjoyed it with a small glass of wine each as we sat and talked for what seemed like hours.

I learned that she loves to go dancing, she hopes to have a house with a big garden someday and that she longs to have children in her life. I told her all about my work at the fire station, my love of coffee and that my free time is pretty much made up of princess tea parties and finger painting.

We laughed, a lot. It was a pleasure to get to know her better, she was exactly the kind of person I thought she was. Sweet, kind and beautiful. I learned about that fire I saw in her eyes, her determination to become a writer and eventually open up a little book shop. She was an inspiration and she really seemed to have her heart set on achieving those dreams one day, I just knew she would do it too.

We finished up our meals and made our way back towards the truck, just as I pulled open the door we both heard music and laughter coming from the bar next to the restaurant. I made the decision easily, I pushed the car door shut and grabbed Sophie's hand.

"Come on," pulling her towards the bar.

"What are you doing?" she said with a giggle, there was no fight in her though as she followed me.

"We're going dancing!" I said with a huge grin.

As we stepped inside the music was pumping, drinks were flowing and the dance floor was heaving. It was only nine thirty at night but everybody was already letting loose and having a good time.

I bypassed the bar and headed straight out to the dance floor, the carefree laughter coming from Sophie was like a drug, I'd do anything to get her to laugh like that again. Her smile lit up her whole face as we came to a stop in the very centre of the dance floor and I pulled her towards me and held her close.

"You're crazy!" she shouted over the music.

"Crazy for you!" I shouted back and felt like the biggest cheese ball on earth.

She just looked up at me with the most beautiful smile, her face radiated happiness. I pulled her closer and we began to move. We danced for what seemed like hours, jumping and spinning, we danced the night away. I couldn't stop touching her and it seemed like she couldn't stop touching me either. If her arms weren't looped around my neck, she was running her hands up and down my chest. I was hot for this woman. I hadn't had this much fun in a long time, we took a few drink breaks in-between dances. Neither of us were drunk, we had only been drinking water but it almost made the night better, there was no buzz pulling us along, it was all us and our amazing chemistry.

The longer the night went on the songs began to change into something more sexy and sultry, I slid my hands down Sophie's beautiful back as she swayed her hips in front of me. Staring into each others eyes, I knew she could see the lust in mine as I could see it reflected back at me in hers. She slowly turned in my arms and pressed her arse into my groin and began slowly grinding into me. God she was hot. My heart was pounding in my chest as I grabbed her hips and held her to me tightly, I ground my hardness into her arse as we swayed to the music.

I was so hard and so turned on I wanted to strip her naked right here and now. Could I do this? I hadn't been with anyone since my wife, was this what I wanted? I knew it was, this was Sophie. The sweetest woman I think I'd ever met, she wasn't just a fuck. What I felt with her was something big, something more than just one night of hot sex. This was something special. That thought was what prompted me to lower my mouth to her ear and say, "Do you want to get out of here?". My voice was so husky I barely recognised myself. I could feel her tremble under my hands as she slowly turned and looked up into my eyes.

"Are you sure?" she asked, hands on my face, I could tell that she was searching for uncertainty. She wouldn't find any.

"I'm sure honey, if you want to?". Oh God, had I misread things, she was married too. Maybe she wasn't ready to move on. Granted she was going through a divorce. I think she could sense my internal panic as she grabbed my hand and began to pull me towards the exit.

Once we got outside and I could hear myself think. I pulled on Sophie's hand gently to turn her around. I gathered her into my arms and held her close.

"I'm sure Hugh, I do want to. But I should tell you that, erm ... Liam is the only man I've ever been with. I'm not experienced, probably not as much as you'd expect from a thirty two year old woman". She seemed embarrassed and there was no need to be, I'd look after her.

"Honey, it's fine. I'll look after you and if there's something you don't want to do or if you decide you want to stop then that's fine too". I could feel her pulse pumping hard in her wrists, she was just as nervous as I was.

"Ok, let's go". Sophie said with a smile.

I led her to my truck and buckled her inside, I was really going to do this. I hadn't had sex in a very long time and now I suddenly couldn't wait any longer.

# Chapter Eighteen

## Sophie

As soon as we walked through my front door and the door was closed and locked, we were on each other. It was like the beast couldn't be contained for another second and we just needed to touch, hold, kiss, caress.

Hugh grabbed me by the waist and pushed me up against the entrance wall, his mouth crashed to mine as he absolutely devoured me. His tongue licked at my lips demanding entry, and of course I opened up and let him in. He kissed like an absolute dream, tender but firm, romantic but dominating. I'd never been so thoroughly kissed in my life.

My hands held tightly to the lapels of his jacket as I dragged him closer, he grabbed a hold of my thigh and brought it up to his waist, causing my dress to rise up to the top of my thighs.

He ground his hardness against my core whilst I writhed in his hold, I couldn't get him close enough.

"I want you," I told him.

"You can have me," he whispered back.

His free hand that wasn't holding my thigh moved down my chest, stroking down from my neck, between my breasts and settled between my legs. He pushed his thumb firmly against my clit over my underwear and I couldn't hold in my groan.

"Is this ok?" he groaned against my neck.

"Yes, don't stop," I moaned into his mouth.

He gently pulled my lace thong to the side and swiped his thick fingers through my wet slit. I was soaking wet. I don't think I'd ever been this turned on in my entire life.

"Ohh ... Hugh" I moaned.

He left his thumb pressing firmly on my clit and entered one thick finger inside me, thrusting gently. I rolled my hips as I ground down against him. He felt incredible.

"More," I pleaded.

He didn't make me wait long as he added a second finger, stretching me. I could feel how hard he was, as he ground himself against my thigh.

He suddenly pulled away, leaving me feeling empty. He brought his fingers to his mouth and sucked them clean with a growl.

Hugh then dropped to his knees before me, pulled my dress up to my waist, looking at me with a silent question in his eyes.

I nodded frantically, he slid his thumbs into the straps of my thong at my hips and lowered them down my legs to the floor as I lifted my feet so he could remove them.

Once they were free from my body he scrunched them in his fist, brought them to his nose and took a deep inhale,

"Mmm holy shit honey, you smell fantastic", he slid my thong into his back pocket,

"Mine". Holy shit, I felt like I was on fire. That was the single hottest thing I'd ever seen, I didn't even have the good grace to feel embarrassed. I just wanted more. The look on Hugh's face was one I'd never seen before. The lust, desire and hunger in his eyes was sending shivers down my spine.

I was still standing shakily, leaning against the wall in the entrance of my tiny apartment, Hugh grabbed my leg and threw it over his thick muscled shoulder. As if watching it all happen in slow motion, Hugh's mouth descended on me. He placed light kisses up my left thigh and then my right. I could feel his warm breath against my bare skin, his nose pressed against my pussy as he took a deep inhale. Holy shit this man was going to kill me.

"Mmm," he moaned before I felt the first swipe of his tongue. He licked from my entrance to slit. Once, twice. My legs were already shaking. His lips pressed against my clit as he sucked and nibbled my most sensitive spot.

I slid my hands into his silky brown hair and clenched my fists and pulled, I couldn't decide whether I wanted to pull him closer or push him away. It felt too good. I'd never felt this intense pleasure before, shit, Liam had never even got me off. I always had to finish myself off in the bathroom.

Hugh didn't give me a second more to think, he made out with my pussy the same way he'd kissed me earlier. My legs began to shake harder, I could feel the pressure building, I was seconds from exploding. White lightning flashed behind my closed eyelids whilst I ground my pussy against Hugh's lips. His fingers were deep inside, thrusting firmly.

"Come for me honey, come all over me". He nipped at my clit and that was it, I exploded all over his mouth. I continued to grind on his face as the warmth spread from my core all the way through my body. I had never come so hard in my life.

As I came back down to earth, Hugh stood and crashed his mouth to mine. I could taste myself on his lips. His cock was so hard it was pushing through his jeans and poking me in the hip. That must be painful.

I tore myself away from his mouth and frantically pulled on his belt buckle, I needed in his pants and I needed inside them right now.

"Honey, you don't have to". He said sweetly, sounding slightly pained.

"Uh uh, it's my turn. Mine". I told him as I lowered to my knees on the carpet. I pulled his belt free from his jeans, undone his button and zipper and pulled them down to his knees.

His erection was straining in his boxer briefs, the tip poking out of the top. I leant forward and licked at the pre-cum beading on the end. Closing my eyes as I let his saltiness coat my tongue.

I reached around and grabbed two handfuls of his firm arse as I brought my forehead to lean against his lower belly. His smell was intoxicating, as his trimmed hair tickled my cheeks.

His hands were caressing my hair, he pulled it together in one hand and held it back, so he could see what I was doing.

I slowly gripped the waistband of his boxer briefs and lowered them to his knees, he kicked them and his jeans off onto the floor and before me was the biggest, thickest, longest dick I'd ever seen in my life. Holy hell, that wasn't going to fit. As if he heard my thoughts, Hugh wrapped his huge hand around the base of his cock and said,

"Don't worry honey, we'll make it fit". I might just explode right now, I couldn't help but rub my thighs together to ease the ache.

I replaced his hand with my own, my fingers unable to touch around his girth. I leant forward to lick his tip, sucking and kissing. Teasing and caressing. Before I opened wide and took him all the way to the back of my throat, I gagged a little as I opened my throat for him.

"Oh fuck, your mouth is so wet and warm". Hugh's head fell backwards on a groan.

I took him almost all the way out before I deep throated him again and again until I had saliva running down my chin. I swiped it away with the back of my hand before bringing my free hand to caress his balls firmly, rolling them in my hand and pulling gently.

I brought him all the way out before licking a long line up the underside of his throbbing cock. His veins were pulsing and the head looked red and angry. Pre-cum pulsing a stream from his slit. I looked up at him, making eye contact before I stroked both hands up the back of his thighs, making sure to drag my nails across his skin. His hard dick bobbing in front of my face.

I rested both hands on his arse and dragged him closer,

"Fuck my mouth Hugh, don't hold back".

I took a deep breath and put his throbbing length back between my lips and hummed. The vibrations turning Hugh feral. He moved both hands to my temples, his large hands holding back my hair as he grabbed my head. Looked into my eyes one final time, a silent question asking if I was sure. I smirked around his length and that set him free.

He pulled my face closer, fucking my face hard. I opened my throat for him, gagging each time he went deep.

"Ah fuck yeah, take it honey, take it all".

I swallowed around him as he brought a hand around my throat, "Do it again,," he groaned.

I swallowed again, maintaining eye contact.

"Ah fuck, I can feel myself in your throat". He held my throat hard, not enough to restrict my breathing. Just enough to hold me in place. He fucked me hard, pumping his hips forward.

I felt him grow impossibly harder, as he began to pull away,

"Honey, I'm gonna ...... I'm gonna". The words died on his lips as I pulled him closer with my hands on his arse. Letting him know that he wasn't coming anywhere but inside me, it was mine. I deserved it.

He fucked forward gently, once, twice. His abs tensed as he flooded my mouth with his warm salty come, letting out a roar. I swallowed it all down. There was so much I had to swallow twice.

It took a few seconds as we both caught our breath. Pulling his semi-soft dick from my mouth. Hugh took my hand and pulled me to my feet. Using a thumb to wipe away the remaining come from the corner of my mouth and swiping it across my tongue. I sucked and nipped as I licked him clean.

"Good girl. That was .... un-fucking-believable".

He crashed our mouths together, not caring that he could taste himself. He gathered me in his arms, hoisting me up. I wrapped my legs around his waist as he carried me towards the bedroom. He was half hard again already, his dick teasing my pussy. I couldn't help but grind myself down on it, I couldn't get enough. I was surprising myself, I'd never been this turned on wanton woman that I was now. Hugh had unleashed something in me.

This was going to be a long, exquisite, unbelievable night and I couldn't get enough of him.

# Chapter Nineteen

## Hugh

I carried Sophie in my arms and gently placed her down on her large king sized bed. It was covered in brilliant white bedding which made her look like she was laying on a cloud. Like my very own angel sent down from heaven.

I followed her onto the bed, crawling on top of her, careful to hold my weight off of her by leaning down on my elbows. When I'd first picked her up I'd felt frantic, like I couldn't possibly get inside her fast enough. Now though, now that I finally had her here, I wanted to take my time. This was a big deal for the both of us, no way was this a one and done for me, and I was pretty sure that it wasn't for her either.

I leant down to catch her mouth again with mine, softly, slowly. Our tongues tangled as she slid both hands into my hair and held me close. She wrapped her gorgeous legs around my waist and moaned softly into my mouth.

She seemed to have gotten the memo and was in absolutely no rush to reach the finish line. She slid her hands from my hair and used her finger nails to scrape across my shoulders and down my back, I couldn't hold back the shiver that edged it's way out. Sophie let out a soft giggle as her fingers continued their path down my body and settled on my arse.

Together, we slowly got shot of the rest of our clothes, she unbuttoned my shirt which I pulled off and threw to the floor and I worked off her gorgeous dress which joined my shirt on the floor. My jeans and boxer briefs were still in the hallway, her panties tucked safely in my back pocket.

When my eyes came back to her body I was momentarily stunned into silence, because holy shit, this woman was incredible. Her body was smooth and soft, her tits were full with soft rosy pink nipples which were so hard they were pointing straight into my chest. I lowered my mouth to take one of her soft peaks into my mouth, licking and flicking my tongue and sucking it into my mouth.

My other hand crept up over Sophie's stomach to rest on her other breast, giving it some much needed attention. Sophie moaned and writhed underneath me, her hands were back in my hair, holding me close.

"Hugh ... ahh ... I need you Hugh".

"I'm right here honey, let's see if you're ready for me shall we?".

I moved one hand away from her breast and lowered it to her pussy. I felt her tense underneath me, holding her breath in anticipation. I looked into her eyes, a silent plea for permission.

She gave me a soft smile and a nod, giving me the green light, I didn't hesitate.

I stroked my index finger through her slit, she was so wet and warm. So ready for me.

"Ah, honey you're fucking soaking for me". I added another finger, gently putting pressure on her clit. Sophie's hips rose off of the bed as she began to grind into my fingers as they slowly circled her most sensitive spot.

She began to pull at my arms, she couldn't get me close enough. Sophie then pushed me back and reached over towards her bedside table, reaching inside the drawer, she pulled out a brand new sealed box of condoms. I couldn't tell you the relief that flickered through me to find them unopened.

She hurried to get the cellophane off the box but just couldn't seem to make her fingers move quick enough. She was frustrated. I knew because I was too. I took the box from her and used my teeth to tear into the packaging, with a huge rip the entire box exploded open and condoms flew out everywhere. I couldn't help but chuckle, we were like two fumbling teenagers, not two thirty some things.

Sophie looked at me with an adorably frustrated glare, although I could see the amusement in her eyes too. She picked up a condom and ripped the foil. Taking it out, she gently pushed me over onto my back and straddled me across my thighs.

She took me firmly in her hand and wasted no time in working me up and down.

"Ahh ... fuck!" that took the chuckle right out of me. I was ready, I wanted this woman more than I'd ever wanted anything in my life. She held my thick cock in one hand and lowered the condom over my hard shaft. She shuffled up the bed so she was hovering perfectly above me. She looked into my eyes and I could feel the unspoken question between us. She was checking that I was sure. I hadn't been more sure of anything in a very long time. I gave her a firm nod and reached for my dick, I first rubbed it hard against her clit and she closed her eyes above me. She was so wet and so ready my dick slid against her easily.

She was grinding her hips, searching for me, trying to get me exactly where we both wanted to be. I pointed the head of my dick to her entrance and Sophie slid down onto me smoothly, she took inch by glorious inch, slowly, savouring every groove and ridge. Fuck she was tight.

When she bottomed out we both let out a deep groan, I hadn't been this close to a woman in years and I felt like I'd died and gone to heaven. Our souls entwined and my whole body lit up with warmth, joy, relief. I couldn't explain it, I felt like I'd found the other half of my soul, I felt like I'd finally found ... home.

"Good girl, Mmm you feel like heaven".

She began to move as I held tightly onto her hips, she ground down onto me. Her warm silky inner muscles were holding me like a vice. Fuck I wasn't going to last long with her on top.

I sat up and swept her beneath me, never leaving her body. She wrapped her legs around my waist, her warm hands tangled in my hair and pulled my mouth to hers. Our kiss was slow, full of passion as I continued to pump into her.

She was moaning into my mouth, pure pleasure radiating off of her. I grabbed her hands and held them together in one of mine, above her head. Which pushed her gorgeous tits right up into my face, I licked and sucked, nibbled and caressed them both. One at a time. Giving them equal attention. I couldn't get enough of her taste, her scent. It would forever be engrained into my soul.

I continued to pump into her slowly, lavishing her body with attention. Whispering sweet words into each others ears, I felt her begin to quiver. She was close. So was I but I needed her to let go first.

Our warm breaths tangled and I lowered my head into her neck, kissing and nibbling on that sweet spot just below her ear and that was it. She went ridged and stiffened below me, moaning my name. Her muscles gripped me, milking my cock, trying to pull me further into her body and that was when I let go. Heat shot down my spine, unfurled in my stomach down to my balls and surged through my body. White hot pleasure tingled through my entire body as I shivered and shook above her. Still pumping my hips, we rode out every single second of pleasure from each others bodies. Until I collapsed against her, recovering from the strongest climax I'd ever experienced. She pulled me closer as we just held each other tightly.

What we just did had been a massive deal for us both, this was the first time I'd slept with somebody since I lost my wife and it was the first time for Sophie with someone who wasn't her husband.

I felt heat behind my eyes and a lump form in my throat, I blinked rapidly, my head still buried deep in Sophie's neck.

My chest was heaving and I tried so hard to hold back my emotions but this sweet angel beneath me just held me closer, stroked my neck and whispered in my ear,

"It's ok Hugh, let it out. It's ok baby".

The flood gates opened and I heaved giant sobs into Sophie's neck, I hadn't cried like this in a very long time. I cried and cried as Sophie held me close, my softening dick had fallen from her now as she held me tightly, running her free hand up and down my back.

"It's ok," she continued to murmur into my ear. It felt like I'd cried for long minutes. As I began to calm down and regain my composure, it was important to me that I explain myself. I raised my head up and looked Sophie in the eyes, they were wet and red rimmed too.

"I'm sorry honey. I need to explain". I hiccupped against her, breathing slowly in and out to calm my body.

"No baby you don't, I understand". She replied as I lowered my head to kiss her soft swollen lips.

"I'm not crying because I'm sad. I'm not crying because of what we just did or because I miss my wife. I'm crying because I feel like I just came back to life. I feel like I've earned a second chance. I never thought I'd feel anything ever again when I lost Grace. But I feel like you just stitched me back together and made me feel whole again".

Her tears began to flow then as soft sobs left her body. We lay together, crying together, holding each other tight as we both finally found peace in each others arms.

# Chapter Twenty

## Sophie

I woke the next morning snuggled next to the hottest man I'd ever met. I was warm, too warm. But I didn't have any urge to move. I slowly blinked open my eyes, Hugh's hard body was pressed tightly against my back. His arm draped across my hip, his big hand pressed against my stomach.

I could feel his deliciously hard erection nestled between my arse cheeks. We were both still butt naked, crashing out after round three last night.

I took a moment to snuggle closer and pull his arms around me tighter. He had full sleeves of tattoos on his arms which I hadn't noticed before last night. They were all in blacks and greys and they were downright porn worthy. I loved a man with tattoos.

It was obvious that he took very good care of himself, bulging biceps, a hard chest with muscled pecs leading down to what had to be an eight pack. I closed my eyes and relived the memories of last night, remembering how that eight pack of abs led down to that delicious set of muscles pointing down to the biggest, thickest, hardest cock I had ever seen.

I mean, obviously I'd only physically been with one other man, but a girl can watch porn too you know. And that cock could rival a lot of those guys!

I was getting hot and horny again and couldn't stop my hips from grinding backwards into Hugh's crotch. He was already hard, a deep sleepy groan sounded from his chest as he flexed his hips, pushing himself into me. No words were spoken, the rip of foil filled the room and then he was there, pushing into my soaking wet heat and taking me to heaven once again.

When we finally made it out of bed an hour later, my muscles were aching, my pussy was deliciously sore and I couldn't wipe the grin from my face.

"So, what are you doing today?" Hugh asked as we worked together to make some breakfast of scrambled eggs on toast.

"Well I'm working this afternoon, but this morning I have a doctors appointment. In about an hour".

"I see, is everything ok?", he sounded unsure of whether to ask or not. I thought it was sweet, I knew he wasn't trying to be nosy, he was genuinely concerned.

"Well, we will soon find out. Erm ... when I was with Liam, we tried to have a baby for a long time. Four years almost, nothing happened. It didn't work. I mean, granted we weren't having a lot of sex. He was always working late or away on business. But something should have happened in that time right?" I looked up at Hugh, who was regarding me thoughtfully.

"I'm sorry, that's weird. To talk about that after what we spent last night doing". I felt the blush creep up my cheeks and I couldn't help but smile. Last night would stick in my memory for the rest of my life.

Hugh stepped forward and grabbed my hands, he pulled me close and kissed my forehead.

"Not weird, you can talk to me about anything. I'm sorry that you've been trying for such a long time to have a child. I can't imagine how hard that must have been. So the doctors appointment is to ...." he trailed off.

"I went to see the doctor at the beginning of the week to get checked over, to see if there's something wrong with me. He agreed that it wasn't normal that I still hadn't conceived after such a long time. Considering I'm still young and healthy. He took some blood and sent it off for thorough testing. I'm seeing him this morning for the results". I could feel the shake in my voice, last night and this morning had distracted me from how terribly nervous I was. What if there was something wrong with me, what if I could never have a child of my own.

"I know this is personal, and this thing between us is very new but, would you like me to come with you?" Hugh asked. He was so selfless and so thoughtful, he wasn't freaking out at all about this conversation.

The whoosh of breath I'd been holding left my lungs and I breathed a sigh of relief. Truth be told, I was terrified of going alone and learning something heartbreaking.

"I'd love that ... really. Thank you", I reached up on tip toes and placed a kiss on his soft lips. He wrapped his arms around my waist and held me close.

"Wait, do you not have to work today? What about Lucie?" I asked.

"I have the day off today. Lucie stayed with my parents last night and they've already dropped her off at pre-school for the morning so I'm all yours".

We arrived at the doctors office a little while later and took a seat in the waiting room. Hugh held my hands which were sweaty and shaking. My tummy was rolling, I was nauseous and I couldn't stop my legs from shaking. Hugh placed a warm hand on my thigh, turned to me and kissed me on the forehead. It was our very first public display of affection but it felt so natural. Like breathing. He brought me calm. I took a deep breath and tried to relax.

Dr Watson appeared in the doorway and called my name "Sophie Taylor, would you like to come in?". I stood and hesitated.

"Will you come with me?" I asked Hugh quietly, I didn't want to push my luck or make him feel uncomfortable but he brought a calm to my soul that I needed at this very moment.

"Of course honey. Let's go. Remember, whatever happens there are options ok, you've got this". He didn't wait for my response, just took me by the hand and led me down the hallway, which happened to feel like he was leading me towards my doom.

"Take a seat Sophie, it's nice to see you. Hi Hugh, nice to see you again, how's little Lucie?". Of course they knew each other, Dr Watson was the only doctor in this tiny town.

"All good Doc, thanks for asking. Let's get to business, otherwise I think Sophie here might pass out from extreme nerves", he gave me a small smile.

"Of course, well Sophie, as you know we took a lot of blood at the beginning of the week. I sent it off for very thorough testing, checking for anything at all which could indicate a reasoning for your trouble conceiving. Now, I'm sure I asked you this at the time, but could you tell me if you have taken any contraception at all in the last six months, specifically the pill?".

"No ... no" I shook my head emphatically. "I came off the pill, hmm ... maybe three and a half, four years ago. I'd been on that pill since I was sixteen. But no, my erm, my husband and I hadn't use any contraception since then".

"I see. Hmm ... this is very odd then. Your blood test picked up a very trace amount of the pill in your system. I know this is a very personal question, but could you tell me when yourself and your husband separated?". Dr Watson's eyebrows were furrowed in confusion, I could tell he was choosing his words carefully.

"What do you mean? Trace amount of the pill? I haven't taken the pill in years ..." I paused, closed my eyes and took a deep breath. I was so confused. I looked back up into Dr Watson's kind eyes.

"My husband and I separated just over three months ago".

"Have either of you ever had any fertility testing in the past?" he asked.

"No, I'd always been too nervous. But I can tell you that there is nothing wrong with my husbands sperm ..." I said angrily. *What the hell was going on?*

"Can I ask how you know that Sophie, if you don't mind?" Dr Watson questioned gently and I heard Hugh suck in a breath. I'd recently told him why Liam and I had separated.

"Well ... I left my husband after I found out he was having an affair ... and had gotten her pregnant". I waited for the familiar sadness to hit me, but it didn't. I just felt angry. If I hadn't taken the pill myself then how did it get into my body?

"I see. I'm very sorry to hear that you've had such a difficult few months Sophie. You've found a good friend here in Hugh though". I knew I had. He was much much more than a friend. His firm grip on my hand, his thumb caressing my palm gave me the strength to ask my next question.

"Dr Watson, I definitely have not taken the pill in years. However, I must ask, how did it get into my system otherwise? It just seems so impossible". I couldn't piece everything together, it just wasn't making sense.

"Well, that's where this gets tricky and I definitely would not like to speculate considering I don't know all the details of your marriage. However, can I tell you a story?". Dr Watson asked carefully, I know he was putting himself out there. He had something to say but had to remain professional to say it. I nodded.

"Well a few years ago, I encountered a similar situation to yours. A couple had been trying to have a baby for a long time, nothing had happened so they came in to get some testing done. The woman was absolutely fine, totally healthy, ovulating well. The man was also fine, a very healthy sperm count. However, when I ran the woman's blood work she also showed amounts of the pill in her system. Her levels were much higher. Well long story short and after a lot of investigating, it turned out that the husband had been slipping contraceptives into the woman's food every day. Now this can lower the effectiveness of the pill working due to the breakdown of the tablet, but it was able to still offer a certain amount of protection. Now, I am in no way accusing anybody or assuming that this is what has happened in your situation. But, and I ask this with all respect and empathy to you Sophie. Do you think your husband could have prevented pregnancy without you knowing? The trace amount in your blood is very low, which would tell me that it's certainly been a few months since the pill was absorbed into your blood".

Hugh's hand squeezed mine, I looked at him. He looked just as shocked as me. I stood and began to pace the doctors office, bringing my hands to my face, the first few silent tears tracked down my cheeks. I didn't even have to think about it, I knew Liam had done it. He had always been very up and down about trying, never seemed overly interested in sex and didn't seem to care either way.

"He did this to me? He took this away from me?" I almost shouted.

The doctor stammered ... "Sophie, we don't know that for sure".

"No," I butted in "He did, I just know it. How else would this have happened. We didn't always eat together so he couldn't have put it in my food. But ...". I stopped my pacing and looked into the doctors kind eyes, how could this have happened. I racked my brain and then it hit me like a ton of bricks.

"My water", I whispered. That had to be it.

"Liam had always been very insistent about me drinking lots of water, he told me it would be good for my body, to help me get pregnant. I always kept a tumbler of water by my bed and regularly drank throughout the night. It was always empty by morning," I told him.

"A tumbler?" he asked. "That could be a possibility, was the tumbler clear?".

"No, it was dark purple. Not see through, I wouldn't have been able to tell if something was in there". Oh God, my husband had been drugging me with contraceptives for years and I'd truly had no idea. It wasn't as if we had regular sex either so it must have been enough.

"Jesus," Hugh muttered, rubbing his hands down his face. "Do you really think that could be possible Doc? I mean would it work?" he asked Dr Watson.

"As I said, the crushing of the tablet would decrease it's effectiveness significantly. However, if sexual intercourse was not regular, or if not done when ovulation had occurred then there is a chance that it could have prevented pregnancy. Sophie, if it's ok with you I'd like to carry out some further tests. The pill won't be traceable much longer but I'd like to check the health of your uterus, ovaries, cervix. Just to make sure that nothing else could have been contributing. Is that ok?".

"Of course, do any tests you feel are necessary. There really could be nothing wrong with me?" I asked on a plea, tears streaming down my cheeks as Hugh held me close.

The doctor stood and walked around his desk, took one hand in his and told me "There's a strong chance that everything is fine Sophie. You're young, healthy. The tests we've done so far show me nothing that would indicate any problems. Let's get these last tests done, just to rule them out". He gave me a kind smile and patted the top of my arm.

"One more thing, and I'm being completely unprofessional when I say this so please do keep it between us. There may not be anything wrong with you Sophie, but there could be something very very wrong with your ex husband". He spoke angrily on my behalf.

"We'll get to the bottom of it," he promised.

Hugh led me from the doctors surgery in a daze. What the hell had just happened?!

# Chapter Twenty-One

**Hugh**

*Dear Sweetheart,*
*I went on a date with Sophie last night. We went for dinner and ended up going dancing too. We had such a good time, I haven't had that much fun since before you left.*
*So, things progressed and I went home with her. I don't know if I should be telling you this. I mean, if you are still out there then I'm sure you would have seen. You were always my best friend so I feel like I can talk to you about it.*
*We went home together, I slept with her Grace. The first woman I've been with since you. It hurt my heart but at the same time, I felt ... free. Like I know now that I'm going to be ok. I truly thought that I'd never feel anything for anyone ever again but there's just something about Sophie. She makes me feel like I can live again, like I can breathe again, like it's ok.*

*I hope I haven't hurt you darling, but I feel like she's stitching my crippled heart back together. She's incredible, so kind and smart. I can't wait to get to know her better.*
*We had an amazing time together... until we got to the doctor's office for her appointment. What an utter shit show that was. Her husband is a piece of shit and I hope for his sake that he never comes face to face with me.*
*Anyway, speak soon,*
*Love Always,*
*H xxx*

I couldn't even begin to imagine what Sophie must be feeling right now. To spend years of your life with somebody and not truly know who they are at their core. The betrayal is huge. When I left her to come to work this afternoon she was very quiet, totally in shock. I can't say I blame her.

I mean, is that even possible? To drug somebody with contraceptives once you've already agreed to have children with them. What kind of arsehole is this bloke? Not only that, but then to get someone else pregnant, someone who is pretty much a stranger. Sophie must be so hurt.

# Chapter Twenty-Two

**Sophie**

It had been a few days since that bloody awful appointment at the doctors and I can't say that I'm any closer to coming to terms with what had happened. I mean, believe me when I say that I am beyond relieved that my body could well be totally fine. I might actually be able to have a child one day. But the fact that my husband, the man I had spent half of my life with and truly thought I knew what kind of man he was, he could have been purposely preventing me from getting pregnant. That's just insanity isn't it, something you see in the movies or read in a book. That couldn't really happen in real life could it? I couldn't get my head around it.

I had a call this morning letting me know that I have an appointment for an abdominal scan on Friday. They'll check my uterus and ovaries and let me know if there's anything else going on. I know deep down in my heart though that I'm fine. I know this was Liam. I know that he did this to me and I don't quite know what to do with that knowledge.

Hugh suggested that I tell my lawyer about it, get his opinion and see what he suggests. Maybe I should, I mean surely it's illegal to be drugging somebody without their knowledge, even if it wasn't something sinister like poison. The thought gives me shivers.

When I told Liam four years ago that I was ready to start a family, he seemed up for it. He wasn't overly excited about the idea but he definitely didn't voice any opinions which would have made me think it wasn't something he wanted. He had never been an overly emotional man so that's just how I took it. He was indifferent, which I now understand he was about most things. If he would have told me that he wasn't interested then I definitely wouldn't have forced him into it, no matter how much I wanted it for myself.

I feel like I don't even know this man, I feel so incredibly betrayed by him. He was my friend, my confidante, my husband, the only company I had half the time. Why didn't he just talk to me? Why go to such extremes? If that's what happened of course, it's much too late for there to be any evidence. The only way I'd know is if he admitted it and I'd much rather never talk to him again. How can you put so much love and trust into someone to find out that they aren't the person you thought they were.

I'm pulled from my depressing thoughts by my phone ringing. I'd just finished my shift at Trudie's and had been slumped on my sofa deep in thought for the last twenty minutes. I wasn't in the right frame of mind to go to the library tonight. I reached into my apron pocket and pulled out my phone, my heart skipped a beat and a small smile finally graced my lips when I saw that it was Hugh calling.

"Hi handsome".

"Hey honey, how are you doing?" He replied in that sexy deep voice of his, it made my thighs clench without my permission.

"I'm good, just finished work, just sat on the sofa considering my life choices," I said with a sarcastic laugh.

"Well ... you decided to give me a chance so it can't be all bad", I could hear the smile in his voice. He had been my absolute rock since my appointment last week.

"That is very true, is everything ok?", I could hear lots of noise in the background on his end, as if he was still at work.

He signed heavily down the phone, "Hmm not really. I was just about to finish work when we had an emergency call come in. There's a fire over at Bedgebury Place and they need all hands on deck". I hadn't been to Bedgebury Place myself but I'd heard that it was in the rougher part of town so I'd kept my distance.

"Oh no," I said, "I hope everyone is alright".

"We will be there soon, we're in the engine now on our way. But, I have a problem Soph and there's no way I'd put this on you if I had another choice. I know that we are still very new but I was wondering if you could do me a favour?".

"Of course Hugh, you know I'll do anything to help. You've been an absolute rock to me the past few days, it's about time you gave me the opportunity to repay the favour".

"You don't owe me a thing honey, but, I was supposed to pick Lucie up from pre-school in about forty five minutes but I don't think I'm going to make it. I'd usually ask my folks but they are off on their pre-Christmas cruise and Freya is busy on shift at the hospital. Obviously the guys are here with me and Lily and Maisie are both held up at work". He was nervous rambling and it was damn cute for a 6'3 burly man.

"Hugh?".

"Yes baby?".

"I'm happy to pick up Lucie, she's a sweetheart. I just hope she won't be too disappointed that it's me picking her up and not her Daddy".

"Oh she will definitely not be disappointed, she's spoken about you non stop since her birthday party and she loves spending time with you whenever we've bumped into you before. But, are you sure? I know you've been working all day".

"Hugh, I love kids. I'd be happy to help, I'll bring her back to mine and keep her busy until you get here". A thrum of excitement swirled in my tummy, I loved kids but I rarely got to spend much time with them. I was already making plans in my head whilst Hugh rattled off the pre-school address and said he'd phone ahead and let them know I was collecting Lucie.

"Thank you so much Soph, I really appreciate it. I'll be with you as soon as I can". Hugh hung up the phone and I hurried to get showered and changed out of my greasy smelling uniform.

I was so eager I made it to Lucie's pre-school 'Little Dumplings' ten minutes early and had to sit in the car and wait.

Luckily the pre-school had a spare car seat that I was able to borrow for such occasions so once I'd installed that I went back inside to collect Lucie.

Now when I say a child's excitement is infectious, I couldn't even begin to describe the excitement that was bursting out of Lucie when she saw it was me bringing her home. She came bounding out the door with her little pink backpack, her brunette curls wild and framing her face. She looked like she'd had a thoroughly good day which made me forget all about my awful few days.

"Sophie! Sophie! I so happy to see you! Miss Angie told me you were coming and I just so excited. She said that my Daddy was stuck at work so you was coming and I so excited. It's the best day of my whole life!", she was rambling just like her Dad had been not too long ago. I couldn't help but smile as I scooped her into my arms and buried my nose in her strawberry scented curls. I couldn't tell if that was the scent of her shampoo or she had actual strawberry in there, so far the only identifiable thing in her hair was paint and I'm pretty sure there was play dough too.

"Yep, that's right kiddo. Daddy is stuck at work putting out a very big fire so you're coming back to my house. How about we have some dinner and then maybe we can do some .......baking!" I built up the word baking because I knew she was about to lose her mind. Every kid loved baking right?

"Oh .... my ....God! I love baking! Daddy doesn't do it very much because he burns everything in the oven. They always come out a bit black but we always eat them because we did try our bestest. Daddy says that's the most important things, that we tried our bestest".

This girl, she was just the cutest little person I'd ever met.

"Your Daddy is right sweet pea, as long as you try your very best then that's all that counts. Let's get you in the car shall we?".

I lowered Lucie to the ground and she reached out for my hand, I held that chubby little hand in mine and couldn't help my mind flashing to the future when one day I might have a little one of my own to do this with. I hoped they were just like Lucie, she was a sweetheart.

So, we'd eaten a dinner of sausage, mash and beans. Lucie's favourite apparently. Now we were about to start on our cupcakes. I reached up onto the corner shelf in my kitchen and brought down my mum's recipe book. I held it close to my chest, this was the very first time I was sharing it with somebody else.

"Lucie I have something very special to show you". I handed her the book which she took hold of very gently and laid down on the worktop, immediately opening the cover and exploring the pages.

"Wow, it's so pretty". Not only did it have written recipes but I'd taken photographs and decorated each page to make it more child friendly. This was the book of my childhood and I couldn't wait to share it with my own children some day.

"When I was a little girl, my Mummy and I used to love baking together. We would do it every single weekend and then we would take our treats around to our neighbours houses for them to try. We lived on a street which mostly had lots of Grandma's and Grandpa's so they were always very happy for a sweet treat. All of the recipes in this book are the ones that my Mummy and I made together. It's very special to me, I'm going to use it one day when I have my own children". Lucie was silent for a few seconds, I could see that little brain ticking as she sorted through her thoughts.

"Sophie, where is your Mummy now?". Not the question I was expecting.

"My Mummy isn't here with me any more, she got very poorly when I was younger, she's in heaven now". I tried to be very careful with what I said, I knew Lucie's situation with her own Mum and I didn't want to cause her any upset.

"My Mummy is in heaven too, she loved me very much you know. But she wasn't strong enough to stay here with me. I can't see her any more but my Daddy says that she lives inside my heart now. Does your Mummy live inside your heart too?". I swallow the lump in my throat and blinked back my tears. This little girl has been through so much, she wasn't old enough to remember any time she did have with her mother.

I coughed to clear my throat as I gathered her in my arms, "My Mummy is inside my heart, always. It's ok for us to miss them because that means that we shared a love big enough to be missed. We are lucky to have had them for the time we did".

"It's ok Sophie, we can miss them together..... Sophie?"

"Yes sweet pea?"

"Do you want to be my bestest friend? I thinks I love you". The heavy weight on my chest pressed down, the lump in my throat increased and I couldn't stop the one tear that fell from my eye. Lucie wiped it away with her tiny fingers, "I would love to be your bestest friend Lucie, I haven't had a best friend in a very long time. Everybody needs a best friend right?".

"That's right. Now I has two bestest friends, you and my Daddy. Do you want to be my Daddy's bestest friend too? He talks about you lots! I think he loves you just like I do". God if I didn't get this girl to stop talking soon she was going to make my heart explode inside my chest.

"That sounds perfect to me," I told her with a smile. "Now shall we get baking? How about some chocolate brownies?".

"Yes!" Lucie shouted and then we spent the next two hours baking, laughing, singing and dancing around my kitchen. I mean, it looked like a chocolate bomb had exploded in here but we were having such fun.

It was now eight o'clock and Hugh still hadn't arrived. Lucie was covered head to toe in chocolate and whatever mystery messes from pre-school. "How about a bath little dirty one?".

"Yes!" she shouted again and bounded to the bathroom. I found her digging through my basket of bath bombs. This girl had so much energy, I don't know how she's still going. I'm exhausted but I hadn't been this happy in a very long time.

By the time Lucie is washed and dried, I see the tiredness begin to seep into her eyes.

"Sophie, I so sleepy," she tells me in her sugar sweet little voice.

"I know sweet pea. I'll tell you what, let's get your hair dried and I'll find you one of my t-shirts to wear as a night gown. Then ... we can make you a little bed on the sofa and you can sleep while we wait for your Daddy. How does that sound?".

"Good," she tells me. Tiredness had hit, which meant the chatter had died down considerably.

Lucie was out like a light as soon as I got her all tucked up on the sofa, before she fell asleep she whispered to me "Night night best friend, I loves you". And I was pretty sure I loved her too.

# Chapter Twenty-Three

## Hugh

It was after ten o'clock before I finally finished at the station and made my way to Sophie's house. I'd been working for around fourteen hours straight and I was exhausted and feeling pretty guilty about leaving Lucie with Sophie for so long. The fire at Bedgebury Place was insane, someone on the bottom floor had left a candle burning while they went out, the cat knocked it onto the carpet and the whole place went up like an inferno, spreading up throughout the whole building. Luckily, nobody was seriously injured but unfortunately so many people have now lost their homes. That's the hardest part of my job, I can deal with the physical strain on my body and the exhaustion that hits but seeing people get hurt or losing their prized possessions and even their entire homes, breaks my heart every time.

I was just pulling up in my truck outside Sophie's when my phone dinged with a text,

> **Honey: Don't ring the doorbell when you get here.
> Lucie is sleeping <3**

Yep, she was now saved as 'Honey' in my phone. I couldn't help myself ok.

I dragged my exhausted body up the steps just as the door swung open. Sophie stood with sleepy eyes and a shy smile, man my heart skipped a beat just looking at her beautiful face. She was wearing a silky burgundy tank top and matching shorts with a big fluffy robe over the top. It was the middle of December after all. I stepped up close to her, making sure I didn't touch her. I stank of smoke and was covered head to toe in dark soot. Sophie lent forward for a kiss and quickly stepped back scrunching up her nose with a giggle.

"Hugh ... you look like a character from one of my dirty books. You are literally what I've imagined in my head. Dirty, sooty, muscled fireman with tattooed forearms knocks on my door in search of help. Mmm yummy," she sighed quietly, closing her eyes with a moan.

I couldn't help the bark of laughter that left me as I leaned so close to her I could smell her raspberry and vanilla scent. I trailed my nose down her perfect cheek, leaving a line of soot in it's wake.

"Is that right? And what does the sooty fireman do when the pretty lady lets him in?" I murmured in her ear, she visibly shivered, her nipples pebbled and pressed against the silk of her tank top.

"Well ... first of all the very stinky fireman takes off all his sooty clothes and leaves them outside the door," she whispered as she began moving the braces off my shoulders and pulling them down my arms.

"Then, when he's only in his underwear ... firstly he takes a very quiet peek at his very cute sleeping daughter. Just to settle his need of knowing that she's ok", she smiles up at me as if reading my mind. She leaves my smoky clothes outside, takes me by the hand and leads me to the sofa.

There's my sleeping angel, safe, warm and cosy dressed in one of Sophie's t-shirts and snuggled up in a huge blanket, fast asleep, a serene smile on her face.

"Then what happens?" my voice was deep and filled with lust, my cock was already straining in my boxer briefs just from Sophie's teasing game.

"Well then I take that sleepy fireman to my shower and I wash his entire body top to bottom, massaging his sore muscles before I lower to my knees and take him in my mouth".

Holy shit, this woman. My cock was so hard it was leaking pre-cum, I couldn't help the groan that left my throat as I followed her like an obedient little puppy towards the bathroom.

Sophie turned on the water and waited until it was toasty and warm before she slipped out of the robe and silky pyjamas, slowly, teasingly. She looked back at me over her shoulder with a smirk, as I skimmed my eyes down her delectable body. Beautiful chocolate hair in waves around her shoulders, skimming the tops of her breasts. Her nipples hard and begging for my mouth. The silky skin of her shoulders and back begging for my tongue to caress down, down, down to her gorgeous round peach. Fuck, I couldn't help myself as I reached out with both hands and took handfuls of her arse, giving it a tight squeeze, leaving two sooty hand prints behind. I pulled her back to my chest and ground my hard length against her arse, I'd never been so turned on. I lowered my boxer briefs with one hand and followed her into the shower. She immediately turned and pushed me under the warm water, filling her hands with her body wash and began working her way down my body. The shower filled with steam and the scent of raspberry and vanilla and my cock was so hard it throbbed. It was painful, in the best way possible.

Sophie worked her small hands from my hair, down my shoulders and arms, across my chest and down to my abs. She caressed down each leg and foot before returning to my lower abs. She squeezed more body wash into her hands, lathering them together into a foam as she stroked my Adonis belt, around to my arse and back again. She was teasing me and I felt no shame when the next word left my mouth,

"Please," I pleaded with a groan. Sophie lifted on her toes and placed a quick kiss on my mouth before she took my cock in both hands, still lathered with her body wash as she began to work me up and down, until the water ran clear.

I groaned in her ear, my hips slowly thrusting into her hand, fuck she felt amazing. This was just what I needed after a long day at work. I stood with my back pressed against the shower wall, water running over my body. My hands were in Sophie's hair as she lowered to her knees and took me in her mouth. Her warm tongue flicked out, licking, caressing my tip before her tongue snaked across the underside of my cock, over the hard grooves and protruding veins. My cock flexed and jumped in front of her face before she opened as wide as she could and took me in one smooth swipe all the way to the back of her throat and swallowed around me.

"Fuck yeah, you're such a good girl, take it all". She hummed around my hard length, there was no way I was lasting long.

I tightened my hands in her hair, pulling her closer before pushing her away, controlling the speed in which she took me. My hips gently thrusting into her mouth.

"Ahh honey, I'm not going to last, you feel too good", I tried to pull out. I didn't want it to end too quickly but Sophie stopped me with a small shake of her head as she smiled around my cock and I couldn't hold back any more. The beast was unleashed and with a grunt I began to move quicker, chasing my orgasm which was already creeping up my spine. Sophie's hands were now firmly on my arse cheeks as she pulled me closer to her, tears were streaming down her face with the exertion as she choked around my cock.

I could feel my dick repeatedly tapping the back of her throat, but she wasn't gagging,

"You're taking me like such a good girl, I'm going to come honey ... here it comes".

My thrusts slowed, my grip on Sophie's hair loosened ever so slightly, Sophie brought a hand up and cupped my balls, gave them a small squeeze and I erupted like a geyser into her waiting mouth. It was never ending as the pleasure spread out through my limbs, my brain went blank, white lights flashed behind my eyes as I groaned deeply.

"Fucking hell," I tried to catch my breath as I looked down and watched her swallow every drop. Her lips were swollen. I pulled her up and smashed my lips to hers, tasting myself on her tongue.

She whimpered in my arms as I held her close, her shoulders were tense and her pupils were blown out,

"I need ... I need", she was so incredibly turned on that she could barely form a sentence.

"I know what you need honey". I switched off the water and led her out of the shower, gathering her in a huge towel, wrapping a towel around my own waist as I began to lead her towards the bedroom. She pulled her hand away, quickly peeking her head around the doorway checking on my daughter. Shit, what was this woman doing to me. Surely she couldn't be this perfect right? I had yet to find a flaw.

She came back to me with a feline smile on her face, throwing her arms around my neck as I dragged her into my body. One quick swipe and her towel was in a heap around her feet. Her body was exquisite, curves in all the right places. Her chest was heaving already and I'd barely even touched her. I reached up my hand and took one breast in my hand as I lowered my mouth to the other. Caressing her perfect pink nipple with my tongue as my hand squeezed the other and I stroked my thumb across her hard peak.

My spare hand began to creep down her tummy to that perfect heaven between her legs, before she moved lightning fast and grabbed my hand to stop me.

"I'm ready Hugh, no more teasing, just fuck me ... fuck me hard!" she looked up at me with pleading eyes, her body shaking with anticipation. My cock twitched, I was already hard again.

I replied with a sharp nod and reached into the drawer in her bedside table and took out a condom, I ripped it open with my teeth and rolled it down my already hard cock.

"Get on your hands and knees and put that gorgeous arse in the air". I'd never seen her move so fast as she obeyed, clambering onto the bed and showing me what was mine. I couldn't stop myself from lowering to one knee and biting her hard right on the arse cheek, she quietly groaned, acutely aware that my daughter was asleep in the next room.

I moved to the other arse cheek and took a bite out of that one too, before moving between her legs and giving her one long swipe from clit to arsehole.

"Mine," I groaned out loud.

"Ah fuck ... Hugh, do that again".

I was only too happy to oblige, I pulled my tongue across her wetness as I pressed my thumb firmly to her puckered hole. I couldn't wait a second longer to be inside her. I stood abruptly, placed a hand on her hip and lined myself up with the other. Thrusting forward and bottoming out in one smooth stroke, her warm pussy clenched around me immediately. She was already so close.

"Fuck me, fuck me, fuck me," Sophie chanted with her face buried into the bedding.

I grabbed a hold of her long, still wet hair, gathered it together and wrapped it around my hand, once, twice as I began pounding into her wet heat.

I kept up my punishing rhythm until she exploded all over my cock, one more thrust and I joined her in reaching nirvana.

Perfection, contentment, true euphoria. We fell to the bed together in a tangled mess of limbs, tired and satiated as I pulled her into my chest and smothered her in kisses before falling into the deepest, most peaceful sleep I'd felt in ... maybe forever.

# Chapter Twenty-Four

**Sophie**

I woke the next morning to the most delicious heat pressed against my back, Hugh was curled around me, every inch of our bodies touching. His snores filling my ear and his warm breath against my neck.

That wasn't what had woken me up though, there was a tiny little hand caressing my face, a tiny little body pressed against my front and the cutest little whispers filling my ears. I couldn't stop the grin that stretched across my face as I cracked open my eyes and was greeted with the most gorgeous big brown eyes. Lucie's face was so close to mine that our noses were touching, her little hands holding my cheeks.

Now that I was awake I could piece together what she was saying,

"I told you my Daddy wanted to be your bestest friend didn't I?" she tells me. The cutest little smile on her face, we didn't quite think through the fact that Lucie was going to catch us in bed together when we collapsed from exhaustion the night before.

"Look, he is giving you big snuggles. He gives me those big snuggles and I'm his bestest friend too".

Hugh's hand flexed on my hip and a low groan sounded in my ear. Lucie kept whispering, unaware that her Dad was waking up and listening to all her secrets too.

"I thinks he loves you just like I love you". she lowered her eyes to the bed, a sombre expression flashed across her face. She moved impossibly closer and said so quietly that I barely caught it "I would like a Mummy like you one day".

Lucie sat back and slapped her tiny hands against her little mouth as though she'd said something she shouldn't have. Hugh hummed against my back and pressed his forehead between my shoulder blades, he had heard her too.

I had to deal with this very carefully, I couldn't say nothing at all, but she is only four years old. I gathered her in my arms and pulled her against my chest, we fit together perfectly.

"Well, you do already have a Mummy sweet pea, remember she lives inside your heart, just like my Mummy lives inside mine. You're Mummy loves you very very much and I know that she would be here with you if she could". I couldn't help the tear that streaked down my cheek. Losing my parents as an adult had been unbearably hard, but at least I got twenty one years with them. Lucie had only gotten a year with her mum and she was far too young to remember her.

"One day, if I'm super lucky and get to have children of my own, I hope they are just like you sweet pea. You're beautiful and kind and you have the biggest heart".

Hugh's huge muscled arm reached around us both, pulling us closer into his chest. His breaths were heavy and I felt a wetness against my back. This poor man, my heart hurt for him. He didn't choose this for himself or for Lucie, Grace didn't choose this either. If I could take away his pain I would.

"I loves you Sophie", Lucie pressed a gentle kiss to my cheek and climbed across me reaching for her Dad. Hugh turned onto his back and held her close to his chest, stroking her hair. Tears were falling freely down his cheeks to his ears and dripping onto the pillow beneath him. I didn't know what to do, I was momentarily frozen. Do I comfort him? Do I give him and Lucie some privacy?

He saved me from my internal panic when he opened those watery blues and with a shy smile he reached out and pulled me to him too.

"Thank you honey", he told me in his deep timber. The last word breaking before he nuzzled his wet face into my hair.

"It's ok Daddy, remember Mummy lives inside your heart too. Me and Sophie are your bestest friends so we lives inside your heart too".

We lay in silence for a few minutes, just holding each other and settling our hearts before Lucie suddenly sat up,

"I think it's time for pancakes from Sophie's special book!". We all broke into a fit of laughter as Lucie bounded off the bed, still wrapped in my t-shirt, and sprinted towards the kitchen.

The next few days seemed to pass in a blur. I worked in the café everyday, spent an hour or two in the library every afternoon and then met Hugh and Lucie for dinner every single evening. It was amazing. I was finally starting to feel like I fit somewhere, like Meadowside could be my new permanent home.

I'd had my follow up appointment at the hospital yesterday. They'd given me an abdominal scan and as I'd already known deep down inside, they found nothing wrong. My uterus and ovaries looked good, healthy and thriving even.

The doctor told me that he had absolutely no reason to believe that I would have any trouble conceiving a child in the future. The relief I felt was immense, Hugh had held me whilst I wept from pure joy.

It wasn't until around a day later when I was out doing some last minute Christmas shopping that the anger started to build to boiling point. If there was nothing wrong with me then it was pretty certain that it was Liam who had prevented me from getting pregnant, even after agreeing to try in the first place. After reassuring me every single month when we got a negative pregnancy test or consoling me when I felt like giving up. He held me as my heart broke every time, when it was him that was putting me through that.

His text messages and phone calls hadn't eased up at all either and I was ready to explode with fury at this man. My rage was simmering just below the surface. He phoned me probably ten times a day, texts were even more frequent. Ranging from sweet messages apologising and begging for me to come home, to issuing me with threats if I didn't. I'd finally caved yesterday and had shown Hugh my phone when he'd heard it buzzing relentlessly in my handbag whilst we were out to dinner with Lucie.

His eyes had lowered to my phone as he scrolled through hundreds of messages. All one sided, I'd only replied to Liam once asking him to leave me alone. I saw the anger flash across Hugh's face. Liam hadn't let up at all and my fury was building and building, couple that with the fact that my very own husband had most likely been drugging me without my knowledge for the past four years and I was ready to explode.

Hugh had encouraged me to get in touch with my lawyer again and fully explain the situation. That conversation is what leads me to right now, sat on my sofa on a Saturday afternoon, surrounded by bags of unwrapped Christmas presents for Lucie and Hugh, a few days before Christmas, waiting for my lawyer to answer the phone.

I spend the next ten minutes explaining in detail about the contraception, my follow up appointments, Liam still refusing to sign the divorce papers and about him relentlessly harassing me. My lawyer said what I had already expected him to, because of the nature of the drugging there would no longer be any physical evidence to prove that it was indeed Liam doing the drugging. The only way we would be able to convict him of anything is if he was to confess and I was pretty sure that wasn't going to happen.

He said that he would look into getting a restraining order filed against Liam which should ward him off until we eventually got the divorce sorted.

Hugh had seen the worry all over my face after I'd shown him the messages. Liam had been threatening for weeks to come down here and find me. Truth be told, I was terrified. This wasn't the man I married, Liam had never been aggressive towards me. Hugh had insisted on installing a camera outside my front door, just in case. He'd also hidden one in the front entrance. He had watched some documentary which taught him that visible cameras can easily be covered up and suggested we have one hidden inside. "Just to be safe," he kept telling me. He had offered for me to stay with him and Lucie but we were still so new and I didn't want to disrupt their family plans over Christmas. I'd be ok, I was pretty sure that Liam wouldn't have the balls to turn up here, he just wasn't that kind of man. He'd never shown much care or concern about anything before.

Before I knew it, it was Christmas Eve. I'd spent the day with Hugh and Lucie on his insistence. We'd been to the Christmas tree light switch on in the town square. We'd enjoyed hot chocolate and spent a few hours socialising with the town folk and our friends.

He had taken the next week off work to spend the holidays with Lucie and his parents. Trudie's was also closed until the day after Boxing Day, which meant that I had the next two days to get through completely alone.

Christmas had always been so magical when my parents were alive. We'd wake up early, exchange gifts before having a delicious breakfast. We'd then spend the day playing board games and watching Christmas movies before Mum and I would start on the Christmas dinner. It was only the three of us but we always had a full spread of food, dessert, crackers, party hats. Mum always made it special, I think it was her way of making up for never giving me a sibling.

Mum had always told me that I brought her enough love that I filled her entire heart. It wasn't until later that I found out that they had struggled to have me and had suffered multiple miscarriages over the years. In the end they were just beyond grateful to have finally managed to have me that they called it a day on having any more, they couldn't deal with anymore heartbreak.

I decided to have an early night so I took my current read to bed, along with a glass of wine to drown my sorrows. I hadn't heard from Hugh since I'd come home and I wasn't expecting to, he had Lucie so he was on full on Christmas Dad mode I expect. Building toys, wrapping presents and getting ready for Santa. I longed for that one day.

Eventually when I finished my book and wine, I fell into an unsettled sleep. I dreamt of my parents, Hugh and Lucie and I even dreamt of Liam. I tossed and turned all night and when I woke on Christmas morning I was beyond exhausted.

I lay in bed for a long time, staring at the ceiling, wondering where things had gone so wrong that I was a thirty two year old woman, almost divorcee, no family, spending Christmas totally alone.

I must have dozed off again at some point after crying myself back to sleep, I was woken a little while later by quiet tapping on my front door and a little voice snaking it's way through the wood that said,

"Merry Christmas bestest friend! Santa has been, open up!".

# Chapter Twenty-Five

## Hugh

I hear footsteps pounding down the hallway towards the door seconds before the door is thrown open and there she stands. Gorgeous green eyes red rimmed, chin quivering, tears threatening to fall.

"What are you doing here?" she whispers, looking from me to Lucie and back again.

Lucie stands in front of me, bouncing on her toes, so excited but desperately trying to hold herself back. Her huge grin is spread across her little face as she reaches back for my hand and pulls me forward towards Sophie.

I reach for Sophie with the other hand and pull her close,

"No one should spend Christmas alone honey, no matter the circumstances. You should never have to spend Christmas alone". Lucie and I moved as one, pulling Sophie into a hug. Lucie wrapped her little arms around Sophie's legs with a giggle.

Sophie heaved a sob into my chest, "Thank you," she whispered. She had been telling me for days that she was fine, she was planning to spend Christmas at home writing her book. Yet as she looked up at me, the relief in her gaze is palpable.

"Look at you both, you look amazing," she says, sniffing back her tears.

I'm dressed in the most ugly Christmas jumper I could find, red Christmas hat with white fluffy trim propped on top of my head. A string of tinsel tied around my neck like a scarf and courtesy of Lucie ... some beard baubles. I know right, believe me they are as ridiculous as they sound but who am I to say no to a four year old.

Lucie is dressed head to toe in an elf outfit, complete with green hat and bell on top of her head, rosy red cheeks and pointy elf shoes.

Lucie runs behind me and brings forward the white paper bag we brought with us,

"We did bring you one too!", she practically shouts at Sophie.

Sophie lets go of my hand and bends down to Lucie's level before taking the bag from her.

"Is that right?" she asks with a huge smile that lights up her whole face.

"And what is it that I'm going to wear?". Sophie reaches into the bag and pulls out a knee length white dress, large white mesh wings and a halo attached to a white headband.

"You're the Christmas angel!", Lucie grabs hold of Sophie's hand, dragging her back inside and ushering her towards her bedroom door.

"Put it on, put it on!". I followed behind and closed the door, making a quick sweep of the entrance to make sure to push the coats and scarves away from the lens of the hidden camera.

By the time I made it into the living room, Lucie was practically vibrating with excitement. She looked like a little elf hopped up on sugar. It had been Lucie's idea to bring Sophie an outfit and by the look on Sophie's face when she re-emerged, it was totally worth it.

My feelings for Sophie were growing rapidly, how could they not, she was beyond perfect. She was smart, clever, generous, thoughtful, she had the biggest heart and my God was she sexy as fuck.

I knew things were changing between us, things were intense and it honestly scared the shit out of me. Sex was one thing but how could I possibly be falling in love with someone else. I'd already given my heart to Grace. It felt like the ultimate betrayal, but I couldn't stop. Sophie was addictive, her taste, her smell, her touch. She set my world ablaze and made me feel more alive that I ever had.

I was enjoying our time together, not just in the bedroom but out in the real world too. She was funny and sweet and she was truly amazing with Lucie.

I needed to shut these thoughts down, for today at least. It was Christmas after all, not the time to be worrying.

Once we had loaded up the truck with all the presents Sophie had bought for Lucie and myself, we headed for home. I had no idea she had bought so much for us, I hadn't received a huge pile of Christmas presents since I was a kid.

We spent the whole morning exchanging gifts, eating breakfast whilst Christmas music played from my phone. We had a gorgeous lunch followed by a Christmas movie marathon. We were stuffed with sweets, crisps, popcorn and fizzy pop. We made it to the second movie before Lucie passed out in a sugar coma on the sofa. Sophie and I spent the next two hours working on the Christmas dinner in the kitchen, working together perfectly. I thought maybe this would feel weird, it had been just me and Lucie for the past few years. My parents always invited us over so we weren't alone but I quite liked spending the day just me and Lucie. We always spent Boxing Day with the folks instead.

The next few hours passed by quickly, filled with good food, good company and copious amounts of laughter. Before we knew it, Lucie was being tucked up in bed after telling us that she had the "bestest day ever!". Me too kiddo, me too.

Sophie and I both fell to the sofa exhausted, holding each other whilst watching the fire crackle in the fireplace. I'd invited Sophie to stay over tonight, it was the first time she'd spent the night at my house.

"Thank you so much for today Hugh, you have literally made today the best day I've had in a long time. I woke up today feeling pretty sorry for myself, I don't have any family. So today was always going to be hard for me. I'm sorry I didn't accept your invitation sooner, I didn't want to be a burden".

"You could never be a burden honey, the last few years have been just Lucie and I on Christmas day. It was nice to have an angel in the house". I smirked at her as I kissed the top of her head, she had long since lost the angel wings and halo. Lucie had claimed them as her own.

She snuggled into me and we just held each other for a while, finding peace in each others company. It had been forever since I'd felt any kind of peace, so I made sure to soak up every second.

"You want to have a shower and then a glass of wine and just relax?", I asked her.

"That sounds perfect".

Whilst Sophie was in the shower, I set up the living room to be a little more ... romantic. Now being a fireman, I wasn't the biggest fan of having lots of candles burning inside the house but I had managed to pick up some battery operated ones at the shop. I set them up around the room. I laid a big fluffy blanket and a few cushions on the floor in-front of the fireplace. I set up wine and chocolate covered strawberries on the coffee table.

Just as I was finishing up, a small gasp came from the doorway and there Sophie stood wearing a silky pink nightdress which ended mid thigh. I could see from here that she wasn't wearing a bra, her hard nipples pointing at me through the material.

"It looks beautiful in here," She whispered.

I walked to her and took her by the hand, leading her towards the blanket and pillows,

"Come here baby". We both settled into the cushions and I passed her the glass of wine before taking a sip of my own.

I let out a sigh, I'd been needing that all day. Christmas with a four year old wasn't for the faint hearted.

Sophie reached forward and took my glass and set it back on the coffee table alongside her own.

She crawled into my lap, placing both legs over mine so she could straddle me. I sat with my back against the side of the sofa.

I pulled her close and nuzzled into her neck, kissing and nipping. She smelt divine.

She reached her hands up and grabbed a handful of my hair as she began to circle her hips above me. I grabbed her hips and pulled her down tightly against my groin, she let out a small moan as she felt how hard I was for her.

I reached both hands up to the straps on her nightdress and slipped them both off her shoulders. Taking a nipple into my mouth, I sucked hard.

"Ah Hugh", she was grinding against the placket of my jeans. My cock so hard beneath that it was trying to break free.

"Take them off," she says whilst pulling at my belt and waistband. She stood and let her nightdress fall to the ground. She stood before me in a tiny red silk thong and I couldn't help but bring my fist to my mouth and bite down.

"Holy shit, you're fucking sexy", I told her as I frantically whipped my belt out of my jeans and kicked them off. Throwing my t-shirt across the room, dressed now in only my boxer briefs I took my seat again against the sofa.

Sophie settled back on my lap and I took both breasts in my hands, squeezing, caressing, flicking my thumbs across her stiff peaks, before taking them one at a time into my mouth.

She moved her hips in small circles, grinding down against my hard cock. I was so turned on a small wet patch was forming on my boxers. I was leaking like crazy.

I reached down and pulled her tiny thong to the side before swiping my finger through her wetness, she was soaked.

"Such a good girl, look how wet you are for me", I told her.

I sank a finger inside her, she was so tight, I could feel her inner muscles clenching around me. I sunk a second finger inside, curling my fingers to stroke against her front wall. She was moaning like crazy, holding onto my shoulders as she rode me. I couldn't wait much longer to sink inside her.

I took the side of her thong in both hands and ripped it from her body, flinging the tiny scrap behind me, I went back to nipping, stroking, grinding.

"Take me out baby," I groaned against her neck. She didn't hesitate, she grabbed the front of my boxer briefs and freed my hard cock from it's prison. She didn't take them all the way off, there was no time for that. She grabbed my shaft hard and caressed me up and down, root to tip, again and again. My head fell back against the edge of the sofa as she worked me. My fingers still stroking inside her with the same rhythm in which she stroked me.

I pulled my hand away sharply, she whimpered in my lap. Her eyes were glazed and hooded, she was as desperate for me as I was for her.

I reached over to my jeans and removed a condom from the back pocket, ripping the foil open with my teeth and sheathing myself quickly.

I grabbed her hips and lifted her above me, positioning myself at her entrance before lowering her onto me slowly. We both let out a groan as I bottomed out inside of her before we both began to move.

She moved her hips in small circles as I thrust mine up into her. The sounds of her wetness filled the room as our skin slapped together. It was like music to my ears, along with our breathy noises and the deep vibrations sounding from my throat.

A sheen of sweat was beginning to cover both of our bodies as we continued to work each other into a frenzy, we were fucking hard and fast now, chasing our releases.

Sophie suddenly climbs from her knees, balancing on both of her feet as she bounces above me, my cock never leaving her.

"Oh fuck, that feels too good. Look at you Soph, taking my cock, fuck".

She continues to bounce as I hold her arse, taking some of the weight off her legs. Fuck me, I'm going to explode.

Her pussy begins to quiver and clench around me,

"Ah Hugh, fuck fuck fuck," then she goes completely still, mouth open in a silent scream, back arching away from me pushing her tits into my face as she comes all over my cock. My dick goes impossibly harder inside her as she milks my orgasm right out of me. I thrust once, twice and then hold still inside her as I release.

I lace our fingers together and hold them against my chest as my orgasm rushes through me and I explode inside of her with a long groan, white spots form in my vision as I pulse deep inside of her.

It seems to go on forever, before my body finally slumps back and Sophie collapses onto my chest.

I stroke my hands up and down her back as we both catch our breath and come back to earth.

My heart is thudding, warmth spreading through my chest as I hold this beautiful woman in my arms, but it's not from the exertion. It's ... more.

# Chapter Twenty-Six

**Sophie**

It was Boxing Day evening by the time I got home. I'd spent the most wonderful day with Hugh and Lucie yesterday, it was like we were reliving my own childhood, doing all my favourite Christmas things. It was so magical watching Lucie enjoy the day, seeing the joy spread across her face when she opened the gifts I bought her was just unbelievable.

Her joy was infectious. Hugh loved his custom made leather bracelet I had designed for him, it was engraved with Lucie's name on the inside. He gifted me a beautiful leather bound notebook, with my first name across the front, it had the most beautiful maple leaf design on the front cover. It was truly gorgeous and I already couldn't wait to use it.

We spent the day today with Hugh's parents, Annie and Paul, otherwise known as Nana and Pop. They were so kind and welcoming towards me, I could tell where both Hugh and Lucie got their loving nature. We spent hours together, chatting, eating, getting to know each other.

Annie even cracked out Hugh's baby albums, much to Hugh's feigned annoyance. Baby Hugh looked so much like Lucie.

I wasn't sure if I'd feel awkward around his family but it felt incredible. I didn't have any family of my own and Liam's parents weren't exactly the warmest of people.

I felt like a part of the family from the very moment I walked through the door and Annie had pulled me straight in for a hug. Hugh must have told them all about me. We'd had a wonderful day.

It was past eight o'clock in the evening before I finally came crashing through my front door, arms laden with gifts, leftovers and my overnight bag. Hugh did offer for me to stay another night but I have the early shift at Trudie's in the morning so I thought it was probably best that I come home. Not that I wouldn't have loved to spend more time with him, he made me feel things I'd never felt before. He made me feel so loved, cherished and completely desired. I was pretty sure that I was falling in love with him, Lucie too. I mean how could I not.

When I was around them both I felt as though I'd finally come home. You know that feeling when you've been away from loved ones for a long while and they just welcome you home with open arms and you finally feel complete. That's how I feel with Hugh, like I've been waiting for him all my life.

There's no way I'd say any of these things to him of course, I didn't want to scare the man away! He was still grieving and I wasn't sure what we were to him, was I just a fling? It definitely didn't feel like a fling, but I was in no hurry to put a label on things. I was just basking in this incredible feeling.

I tidied away all my gifts, finding them all a new home. Put a load of laundry in the machine and took myself off for a shower. It had been a very busy couple of days and I was ready for an early night.

It was barely nine pm when I crashed into bed and was out pretty much as soon as my head hit the pillow.

Something woke me, I couldn't quite place what it was but something deep in my soul had woken me, telling me that something was very wrong.

I stretched out in bed, I couldn't. *What the hell.* I couldn't move my arms, my eyes flew open as I frantically looked around the room. I still had that heavy fog of sleep laying over me, making it difficult to place what was going on and where I was.

I took a deep breath, trying to steady my frantic breaths. I was still in my bedroom, it was now dark outside. I glanced over to my alarm clock on my bedside table which showed it was four am. At that moment, my brain woke up enough for me to realise why I couldn't move.

I looked up to find both of my wrists handcuffed to my bed frame, I was laid out on my back, my legs were free but my arms were spread so wide I couldn't move.

What the hell was going on,

"Hello?" I tentatively called into the dark apartment.

"Is anyone there?".

As I tried to calm my breathing, my pulse thumping in my ears with fear, I began to hear a shuffling coming from outside my bedroom door.

Footsteps sounded, shuffling, almost like something was being dragged. My bedroom door was closed but that didn't stop the noises from reaching my straining ears. A thump sounded, then another. Like something was banging into the walls.

Whoever it was, was coming closer. Slowly coming towards the closed door. My body was shaking uncontrollably, my breaths coming fast and frantic, tears streaming down my cheeks. I felt like I was in a horror movie. You know that moment when the bad guy is coming but you just can't get yourself free.

I pulled hard on my restraints, kicking my legs hard against the mattress. Trying to find purchase to push myself up the bed. I couldn't move, not even an inch. My wrists were burning, the metal of the cuffs causing red, raised welts to appear on my skin. The more I pulled against them, the more my wrists screamed in agony.

I closed my eyes tight, still hearing the shuffling in the hallway seconds before my bedroom door flew open. I was stunned silent. My eyes could not believe what they were seeing. I could barely recognise the person in front of me. Dark brown muddy boots were on his feet, shoelaces untied. Dirty, scruffy navy jeans on his bottom half. They looked like they hadn't seen the inside of a washing machine in a very long time, rips in the knees and what looked like vomit staining his trouser legs. He wore a dark grey long sleeved t-shirt, covered in stains, sweat marks ringing around under his armpits.

But what was truly unrecognisable was his face. Pale blotchy skin, a scruffy unkempt beard, he had large purple circles underneath his sunken in eyes. His dirty blond hair, greasy and sticking close to his head.

In his hand he held a large almost empty bottle of whiskey, which he swung up to his cracked lips before taking a long gulp.

"Hi honey, I'm home," he croaked, his speech slurring. I couldn't help but cringe at the endearment, it sounded so different coming from his mouth.

"Liam?" I whispered. My brain couldn't quite comprehend that this man in front of me was technically my husband. I'd never seen Liam anything less that perfectly groomed at all times. He was always clean shaven, hair perfectly styled, he was always dressed smartly. This man standing in front of me, was not him.

"Yeeees baby, it's mee. I've come to take you h-home". He stammered, barely able to hold up his own weight as he dragged himself further into the room. I now understood the shuffling noise I'd heard before, he could barely walk, dragging his boot clad feet across the floor.

The bed dipped as he sat himself down on the bed. Taking another large gulp from his bottle.

"W-where have y-you been all d-day? I've b-been waitinnnng for you," he slurred. He turned around and grabbed my knee tightly, the revulsion hit me instantly. His hands were cold and clammy, he was squeezing me too tightly. I tried to pull away from him but he just held on tighter.

"Y-you know I saw you g-get out of a t-truck outside earlier. Are y-you fucking that g-guy?". What? He'd been here when I got home earlier. How did I not notice? How did I not sense him?

"Liam, what are you doing here? We have been separated for months now. You have a family waiting for you at home remember. You didn't want me then, you cheated on me". I tried to keep the tremor out of my voice but to be honest, I was quite frankly terrified. This man sat in-front of me was not my husband, his pupils were dilated, the stench coming from him was making it very difficult not to retch.

He placed his bottle down on the carpet between his legs and turned fully to face me. I tried to hold back the flinch that came from me as he turned closer, but he noticed.

"B-baby, I-I made a mistake. I shouldn't h-have cheated on you with Tara. I t-tried to make it work b-but ..." he paused and put his head in his hands.

"What Liam? What happened?", I lowered my voice, trying to sound caring. At this point I'd do just about anything to stop him from getting angry. The wild look in his eyes was terrifying and I felt like one wrong word would set him off.

"The baby isn't m-ine. He isn't mine S-Soph. I threw away my wife, I-I threw you away f-for a woman who was sleeping with s-someone else too".

If I could face palm I definitely would, my marriage is over. My husband spent months cheating on me with another woman and then chose her and their child. Then as it turns out, she was sleeping with other people too, what an absolute joke. I couldn't bring myself to feel one ounce of sympathy for him, he'd brought this on himself and what he had done to me was much worse. What did he expect, that he could just come here, tell me what happened and I'd go skipping off into the sunset with him. He was deluded.

141

I was livid, but still not in the position to try and piss him off.

The more he spoke, the clearer his speech became, as if he hadn't spoken in a long time and he was having to learn again.

"I want you to c-come home Soph. You don't belong h-here. I'm sorry ok? We can f-fix this, I'll never hurt you ever a-again. We can k-keep trying to have a b-baby of our own and it'll be all b-better. Yeah?".

The red hot fury that flew through my veins then, the reminder of what I'd discovered at the doctors office flew to the front of my brain and the words left me before I could think about my current predicament.

"Try for a baby? Try for a fucking baby? Are you being fucking serious right now Liam". I was shaking with pure rage, self preservation flew out of the window. Liam just sat completely still, eyes squinted and head tilted to the side as if he didn't understand the issue here.

My voice came out quiet and deadly then,

"I know what you were doing to me Liam. I know you were force feeding me contraception, you'd been doing it for years! Hadn't you?".

I vaguely remembered the CCTV camera outside in the hallway, my bedroom was close to the front door. I wondered if sound could be picked up, would the camera pick up our conversation if I could get him to confess?

"What do y-you mean Soph? We tried f-for a long time. R-remember we just figured that s-something was wrong with you?". He nodded then, with a leering smile as if he hadn't just said something completely offensive.

He was swaying where he sat, I was amazed he was still upright if I'm honest. He wasn't just drunk, I could tell, he had taken something. A lot of something.

"Something wrong with me?" I huffed an unamused laugh.

"There was nothing wrong with me Liam. And there is no way I'm going anywhere with you, especially if you can't even tell me the truth!", I shouted in his face, spit flying from my mouth.

Liam moved closer, leaning across my legs. I could feel his putrid breath against my inner thighs. I couldn't help but stiffen, clenching my thighs together tightly.

"Ok, ok. You want t-the truth? The t-truth is, I never wanted to p-put a baby in here", he tapped on my sex with his index finger. I shivered in revulsion.

"Don't touch me," I growled. I couldn't fully see his face any more, his head and dirty hair laying across my thighs.

He laughed at that,

"You're my w-wife, I can touch you a-any time I want. And yeah yeah yeah, so I p-put pills in your water. So what? Why d-did I have to have a b-baby if I didn't w-want to. You only fucked me to make a b-baby. I didn't even c-come half the time b-baby. It wasn't baby t-time yet. You get me?".

Fuck, this guy was insane, completely off his rocker. He was so far removed from the man I married, he was like a totally different person.

I swallowed my sob, I'd spent years suffering the heartbreak of not being able to have a child. It was starting to feel like a blessing now though, there wasn't a chance in hell I'd want to have a baby with this bloody lunatic.

I had to play along though,

"Liam, we agreed together to have a baby. I didn't force you into anything. You are the reason for my heartbreak, my depression. I longed for a baby and you lied to my face every damn day of your life!".

"You want a b-baby? Come on then. I'll p-put a baby inside you r-right now!". Liam moved unsteadily onto his knees, he was clawing at my panties trying to get them down my legs.

"No! Get off me!". I kicked and shouted as if my life depended on it, trying to fight him off.

"Get your grubby hands off me you piece of shit!". I bucked my hips and kicked blindly at him. My shoulders and wrists screaming in pain.

He managed to get my panties off and flung them behind him. He grabbed a hold of both of my legs and lifted himself up to sit on top of them. He was so heavy, I'm totally screwed. That didn't stop me from putting up the fight of my life.

"Will y-you shut the fuck up! You w-want a baby, I'm giving you a baby!". Liam reached across the bed, took a hold of my dressing gown and pulled the cord through the loops. He forced it across my screaming mouth and tied it tightly around the back of my head. I screamed into it but the sound was muffled.

I didn't know what to do, he'd won. But I couldn't resign myself to letting him take me without a fight. He looked down at me through his sunken, beady eyes and all I felt was hate.

I hated this man down to my very core in this moment. But the saddest thing was that I'd once loved him so intensely. That man was gone now. He was so drugged up and pumped so full of alcohol. I decided that my only chance was to knock this fucker out.

He sat back on his haunches, grasping at his belt, pulling it through the loops and unbuttoning his jeans. He reached into his boxers and pulled out his hard cock, I gagged and retched around my dressing gown gag. He was revolting. I can't believe I'd ever found this man attractive.

He used his hand to pump his length as he began to crawl backwards on his knees to free my legs.

"Come here b-baby, look how hard I a-am for you. Let's make a b-baby shall we?" he crooned.

My legs were now free from his heavy weight, I held my breath and waited for the perfect moment. I threw a glance over at the clock, it was now five am. I was expected at Trudie's at six to help open up.

Liam began to wobble closer, raising my legs up to crawl between them. This was my moment, I couldn't let him go any further. In one swift move I brought both knees up to my chest, as close as I could get them. I needed the most amount of leverage I could manage. He wobbled in his spot, no longer supported by my legs. I threw my legs forward as hard as I could, smashing both feet hard into Liam's face. I heard a massive crunch as blood exploded from his nose, pain ricocheted up my calves as I brought my legs back up and continued to kick with all my might.

After the third kick, Liam began to sway, his eyes rolled into the back of his head. He fell forwards and landed with a thud, right on top of me. He was knocked out cold, he was beyond heavy. His dead weight laid across my torso. His head landed next to my shoulder, his chest pushing into mine, his disgusting naked cock pressed against the bed between my legs.

Fuck, I did it. If I could move my chest enough to breath out a sigh of relief then I would.

I mean, this definitely wasn't my preferred position to be in but he was unconscious. I was still handcuffed to the bed, dressing gown cord still tightly wrapped around my mouth and head. Liam's warm blood trickling down my shoulder onto the mattress below me. I could barely make a noise.

But I had to have faith that when I didn't turn up for my shift, someone would come looking for me. I just had to wait. I told myself to breathe, just wait and believe that people here cared about me enough to sense something was wrong.

My mind wandered to Hugh, in my mind I called to him. *I need you Hugh, please save me, please. I love you ...*

# Chapter Twenty-Seven

## Hugh

Lucie and I were laid snoozing in my bed on Thursday morning, we'd had such a busy few days we were both totally wiped out. Lucie had made her way in here at six am, turned on cartoons and promptly fell back to sleep.

I was dozing, as much as you can with cartoons blaring in the background, when my phone began to ring. I looked over to my alarm clock, hmm it was only seven am. Too early for one of the boys to call, not that they often did. Too early for my parents to call, unless ... something was wrong. Panic spread though my body at the thought and I lunged towards my still ringing phone.

The caller ID showed that it was Trudie calling, now that definitely didn't happen often. She only called when she needed something fixing and didn't want to call the handy man.

I scrubbed a hand down my face as I sat up and leaned back against the headboard, before answering the phone.

"Hello?"

"Morning Hugh, it's Trudie. I'm so sorry to call you early on your day off", her voice trembled, like something wasn't quite right.

"It's fine Trudie, is everything ok?".

"Hmm, you know I'm not sure sweetie. I know how you and Sophie have gotten close and I didn't know who else to call. Is Sophie with you?"

Alarm bells started ringing in my ears as I slowly pulled back my bedding and pulled myself out of the bed. I quickly walked out of my bedroom door and took a seat on the top step so I didn't disturb Lucie.

"Erm .. No, she's not here. I dropped her back to her apartment last night. She said she had the early shift with you this morning. Is she not there?" I asked, trying to keep the panic at bay.

"That's right, she was supposed to be here at six o'clock this morning to help us get ready for opening. She's usually here right on time, so when it hit six fifteen and she hadn't arrived I went up to the apartment and knocked. There was no answer, her car is still parked outside. I left it a little while and then went back and tried again, but there's still no answer Hugh. I thought she may be with you and that maybe you'd both overslept?".

"No Trud, she's not here. I've not heard from her since around nine last night, she text to say she was having an early night". The panic was building. Nerves swirling in my stomach and making me nauseous. I was racking my brain, where could she be? She wouldn't have left to go somewhere without letting me know, she knew that Lucie and I were coming in for breakfast this morning.

I was trying to sort through my jumbled worries when it hit me, *Liam*. Fuck! I was up on my feet and rushing back into my bedroom to get changed as fast as I could.

"Trudie, I'm coming down. Right now. Sophie has been getting some ... messages from her ex husband. I'll call my parents to come and watch Lucie for me and I'll be right there. Ten minutes tops ok?!"

Luckily my parents lived on the next road so they could be here quickly. I quickly shot off a text to Dad before I scrambled to put on my joggers and t-shirt before making my way downstairs. I was just lacing up my boots and grabbing my car keys when Dad came bounding through the door.

He took one look at my panic stricken face before he moved aside and firmly said "Go", pointing to the open door.

I ran to my truck and was flying out of the driveway seconds later, I was in full on panic mode and had to try and remind myself to calm down and breathe. *Inhale, Exhale, Inhale, Exhale.*

My heart was going nuts as I arrived outside Trudie's minutes later, I threw the truck into park and stumbled out the door. Trudie was waiting outside the café, face as white as a ghost, unshed tears filling her eyes.

I gave her a stern nod before I ran past her and took the stairs up to the apartment two at a time. I pounded on the front door and pressed my ear close to the wood.

"Sophie, honey are you in there?" I called through the closed door. My eyes caught on the CCTV camera outside the door, it was hidden behind a hanging plant.

"Sophie? Are you in there?". I pressed my ear against the door again and closed my eyes, straining to listen for any small noise. That's when I heard it, a whimper, a moan, a cry.

I reared back as far as I could and brought my heavy boot down hard on the door, kicking with all my strength. The wood began to splinter,

"I'm coming baby, hold on, I'm coming", I pounded the door relentlessly as it began to crack and break. One more kick and the door flew open, I bounded inside and began to frantically look around the living room.

"Baby, where are you?" I called out.

Moaning came from the closed bedroom door, I moved swiftly, bowed my head and took in a deep breath. I wasn't sure what I was about to walk in to but when I turned the door knob and swung the door open, the scene was like something from a thriller movie.

Sophie was tightly bound to the headboard of her bed.

She had her robe belt tied tightly around her head, in her mouth. I moved my eyes up to look into hers, they were red, blood shot and she had tears streaming down her face. Her eyes bore into mine, pleading for help.

The most shocking part of this scene was the half naked man slumped against her chest, jeans undone and around his arse, along with his boxer briefs. White arse in the air, flaccid dick pressed into the mattress. That's when I noticed that Sophie had no underwear on, I looked down finding them on the floor by my feet.

In that second I saw red, fury raced through my body and I snapped. I marched forward, reaching Liam in three steps, grabbed him tightly by the back of the t-shirt and pulled him off of my woman. *My woman.* His dirty, half naked body flopped back against my chest before I threw him to the floor with a roar.

He didn't even flinch, didn't make a noise. Was he dead?

I only gave myself a second to think about that before I was on the bed, pulling Sophie's nightgown over her to protect her modesty.

She was sobbing, tears streaking down her cheeks, her chest was heaving as she struggled to take in a breath. I immediately reached for the robe belt that was wrapped around her head and gently began to unwrap it. My rage was making it hard to be calm, but for her I was trying. Her face must be so sore.

I got it free and Sophie let out a howl of agony, relief, sheer pain.

"It's ok honey, I'm here now. I'm going to get you free ok". I stroked a hand down her cheek, wiping away her tears. The sight brought a lump to my own throat.

I moved back and jumped off the bed in search of the handcuff key, the bastard must have it on him somewhere.

"No," Sophie shouted, "Don't leave me, please don't leave me". Her voice cracked, her words coming out quiet and hoarse. I immediately went back to the bed and climbed on beside her. I took my face in my hands and moved my face close to hers. I kissed her cracked lips gently and whispered,

"I'll never leave you baby. But I need to get you free". She gave me a small nod, followed by a shuddery cry.

I heard footsteps coming down the hallway, "Hugh?" a voice called seconds before Ace appeared in the doorway.

"Holy fuck!" he exclaimed. He let the sight before him hold him frozen for all of five seconds before he let out a deep breath and rolled his sleeves up,

"Your Dad text me. How can I help?".

"Check that bastards pockets, we need the handcuff key," I nodded down to Sophie's still unconscious ex husband lying in a heap on the carpet, arse out, cock out, mouth hanging open, completely fucking oblivious to what was going on around him.

Ace walked over to him before checking his jeans pockets with a grimace,

"Fuck," he said. "That is not an attractive sight". He found the key quickly before throwing it to me on the bed. I caught it and began working on the cuffs. Sophie was in a really awkward position, her arms pulled so tightly and twisted at an angle.

While I worked quickly on the hand cuffs, the bed dipped beside me as Ace climbed on to the bed. He covered Sophie with a thick blanket and sat close to her head, he was comforting her, wiping her tears as she pressed her face against his hand. The sight alone caused a tear to leave me and fall down my own cheek.

I'd never seen Ace's loving side, he was always the joker. Flirting with everyone, never taking anything seriously. It warmed my heart to see my friends loving Sophie, she needed all the love she could get.

Sophie began to shiver, her body convulsing violently. Ace brought the blanket tighter around her body, tucking it right up to her chin and began rubbing her arms trying to bring her some warmth.

Finally, a click sounded and Sophie's right arm fell from the handcuff and landed on the bed with a thump.

"I can't feel it," she whispered.

"Baby, they just need to get their blood flow back, they were stretched so far. We'll get you straight to the hospital as soon as you're free ok" I promised.

Ace took her free arm in his hands, he bowed his head seemingly having trouble keeping his emotions at bay. The blood around Sophie's wrists was crusted, but the freeing of them had caused them to start bleeding again. Small beads of blood were welling across the wound as I tried to work faster.

"Soph do you have a first aid kit?" Ace whispered, stroking her cheek.

"In the b-bathroom," she croaked.

"I'll get it", another voice sounded from just outside the bedroom door. Seconds later Lily appeared in the doorway, dropping the first aid kit to the floor in shock. Bandages spilling out across the floor.

"Oh Sophie, oh my sweet Sophie," Lily choked on a sob but quickly pulled herself together enough to scoop up the bandages and join Ace on the bed. They worked together to bandage Sophie's wrist just as I managed to free the second one. It was in no better condition than the first, Ace and Lily quickly wrapped it before each placing a kiss on Sophie's head and leaving the room together and making a call for an ambulance and the police.

I sat on the edge of the bed and gathered Sophie into my arms, pulling her into my lap, tightly wrapped in her blanket. She let go then, she sobbed into my chest, breaths heaving as she clutched at my shirt with her bloody hands.

We sat like that for a few minutes, Sophie in my lap as I tried to warm her and stop her shakes. A tear slid down my cheek without my permission. How could somebody do such a thing and to such a sweet soul like Sophie.

"Hugh?" Sophie croaked, her voice almost completely gone.

"Yes honey?".

"Thank you for saving me," her body shuddered.

"I'll always save you honey, the ambulance and police will be here soon".

"Ok," she whispered.

"Hugh?"

"Yeah?"

"Can you help me put some underwear on before they get here?"

"Of course baby". I placed Sophie down gently on the bed before reaching into her chest of drawers for some underwear, some joggers and a thick jumper. I came back to her and knelt down in front of her.

"I'm going to unwrap the blanket, just for a minute ok?".

She nodded and lifted her hips so I could move it out from underneath her. I moved her legs into the holes of her underwear and began to pull them up, I looked down to see what I was doing when I paused. A sob left my mouth before I could stop it. Sophie had clear fingerprint bruises on the insides of her thighs, dried blood that had come from the crescent shaped nail prints carved into her skin.

I continued pulling Sophie's underwear up, her joggers and jumper next before crouching in front of her. I took her hands in mine and placed my head in her lap. She let go of one hand and used the other to stroke my hair. I couldn't bring myself to look at her as I asked my next question, I didn't want to see the pain and heartbreak in her eyes.

"Honey?"

"Yeah," she whispered.

"Did he, d-did he, you know?".

She knew what I was asking immediately. She used her fingers to push up my chin so she could look into my eyes.

"No he didn't. He didn't do anything like that. He was going to I think. But I kicked the shit out of his face and knocked him out before he could". The side of her lip quirked, as if she would smirk if her face wasn't so sore.

"Thank God," I murmured.

I heaved a giant sigh of relief before I picked her up and tucked her head under my chin, before taking her into the living room.

Sirens sounded in the distance, coming closer and closer as I sat down with Sophie on the sofa. Her in my lap. I didn't want to let go of her again.

Ace and Lily were still there, Ace brought us both over a cup of tea as the emergency services came bounding into the apartment and got to work.

Paramedics worked on Sophie, deeming that she needed to go to the hospital to have some stitches in her wrists and a thorough check up of her arms and shoulders. She had been restrained so tightly and stretched so far for such a long time, they needed to make sure nothing was fractured, dislocated or damaged.

We sat stock still when Liam finally woke up and was led out of the building in handcuffs.

"Sophie?" he howled.

"Where's my wife?"

152

"I need my wife".

We didn't even acknowledge him, we kept our backs turned, Sophie snuggled into my chest. Let him see his wife in the arms of another man, receiving comfort and love from someone who wasn't him. He didn't deserve a second of her time.

Sophie deserved the whole world and he deserved to rot in a prison cell with only his fucked up thoughts to keep him company.

# Chapter Twenty-Eight

## Hugh

It was four hours later when we finally left the hospital. Sophie had been poked and prodded, had x-rays and examinations. She had strain in both shoulders after being held in such an awkward position for so long. Her ligaments over stretching and beginning to tear. We had instructions to ice her shoulders a few times a day and take it very easy. It would be pretty painful for a while. She also needed to have some stitches in both wrists, the handcuffs had rubbed and ripped so far into her skin, I couldn't bare to think about the the pain that she had endured. All while I was tucked up in bed oblivious.

Sophie had been prescribed a weeks course of antibiotics due to her wrist injuries and we had to change the dressings twice a day for the next week.

Sophie was quiet, worryingly quiet. She had barely said a single word since being taken to the hospital. The only time she spoke was when the police came by to ask for her statement. Listening to her account of what she'd been put through was harrowing. I wish

I'd beaten the shit out of that waste of space before the police had arrived and taken him away.

Sophie had barely stopped shaking, trembling with adrenaline and fear. She gripped me tightly and hadn't let go. I'd sat beside her and held her through all her assessments and treatments, whispering words of encouragement in her ear. She was a warrior and I wasn't going to let this bring her down. It was over, the months of harassment, the living in fear of Liam turning up. It was over. He was in prison and I was pretty sure he wouldn't be coming out any time soon.

We walked through my front door by mid afternoon. I hadn't even given Sophie the choice of going back to her house, I knew it wasn't an option right now and there was no way I'd put her through more turmoil. Lily had been by and dropped off a bag of Sophie's belongings, clothes, toiletries and things, while Ace had replaced her front door.

I helped Sophie to take off her coat and shoes before leading her towards my large grey L-shaped sofa. Lucie had insisted on 'decorating' it with large fluffy white pillows and I was thankful for that now.

Sophie immediately laid down and I covered her with a blanket.

"You're ok honey, you're safe now. Let's get the fire going shall we?".

She nodded weakly, I could see the exhaustion beginning to weigh down on her body, her eyes were heavy, purple circles lying beneath them.

I ambled over to the fireplace, quickly getting a fire going to warm up the house. It was nearing the end of December now and it was bloody cold.

"I'll just go and pop the kettle on, get us all warmed up ok?".

Another nod. Sophie closed her eyes and burrowed herself into the pillows. I thought I'd seen pain in her eyes the day I met her, but that was nothing compared to the agony I saw in them now. To be so deeply betrayed by a loved one, how do you get past that?

I busied myself in the kitchen, tidying up the breakfast things left by my Dad and Lucie, whilst I waited for the kettle to boil. He had taken her over to their house to stay for a couple nights.

I wasn't sure what state I would be bringing Sophie home in and for now, that wasn't something I wanted Lucie to witness.

Although, I knew that little girl had healing powers, Sophie would be needing her light and love in a few days time. Children seem to have the innate ability to open your heart and let the joy in, to allow you to soak up the goodness they exude and let it fill you up.

The tea was ready and as I made my way back towards the living room, the noise that filled my ears was enough to break my heart clean in two.

The scream was animal like, desperate, broken, pained. I rushed to put the mugs on the table and gathered Sophie immediately in my arms. She didn't need my words right now, she just needed to be held. Tears welled from deep inside and coursed down her cheeks, like raindrops running down your face on a rainy day. Her body heaved and shook with the force of her heartbreak as she clung to my chest and unleashed her agony.

A solemn tear fell down my cheek, to the outside world my body was calm, but that was only a disguise for how tangled my mind was.

"It's ok baby, let it all out. I'm here, I've got you".

After what felt like hours, Sophie's tears slowed, moans escaping her lips in hiccups. She took a deep cleansing breath as she pulled her head back to look into my eyes. She wiped away the tears that had collected on my chin and leant forward to kiss my cheek.

"You're a good man Hugh Weston, I don't know what I would have done without you today. You saved me, you came for me when I needed you the most and I'll forever be thankful for you".

I pulled her close, kissing her on the forehead, closing my eyes.

"Always," I whispered as my eyes grew heavy. We both fell into a restless sleep, tucked in each others arms, holding each other together. Safe.

It was a few days later when I started to see Sophie's resolve strengthening. Each day she was getting stronger and stronger, not only that but she was getting angry about what had happened to her.

Her heartbreak was dissolving into pure fury. She came to me on Sunday evening after her shower and snuggled into my side on my king size bed. Wearing one of my huge t-shirts that stopped mid thigh. She looked good enough to eat, but there was no way I was going to initiate anything. I was a very patient man, I could wait for intimacy but I'd be lying if I said I didn't miss her. I missed her smell and her taste. I missed the feel of her wrapped around me. Her warmth, her little moans. I missed ... her.

"Hugh?"

"Yes baby," I responded, leaving my wayward thoughts where they belonged, in my mind.

"So I've been thinking," She paused and took a deep breath.

"When I was ... tied up and Liam was doing ... what he was doing. I had a thought. Before he started taking his clothes off and becoming aggressive, we had a conversation. He admitted what he'd done to me with the contraception. He admitted it Hugh. He told me it hadn't been 'baby time'". She used her fingers to create air quotes.

"Jeez he's such a piece of shit, I wish I'd punched him in the face," I muttered. Sophie giggled and it was the most beautiful sound I'd ever heard.

"Me too," she said "But, what I'm getting at is that he admitted it, loud enough to maybe be picked up by the camera in the hallway? I made sure I spoke loudly when I questioned him. What do you think? I totally forgot to mention it to the police that day, things were intense". She questioned shyly, waiting for my response.

"You my love are an utter genius! You spoke loudly on purpose? Questioning him in the hope of getting evidence? How on earth did you manage to end up with that fucking dick?".

I pulled her gently onto my chest, as she huffed weakly "He wasn't always a dick". I made sure not the pull on her arms, they were still very tender. She laid down on top of me, head to chest, tummy to crotch, legs to legs. She was so much smaller than me, but we seemed to fit together perfectly.

"You think it might have worked? I want to press charges Hugh, he is not the man I married. Liam had never hurt me before. He'd never even raised his voice to me. He was always just ... indifferent to me I suppose". She said with an involuntary shrug of her shoulders and then immediately winced.

I brought my hands to her shoulders and gently massaged them, just the warmth from my skin to hers seemed to lessen the pain just slightly.

"I think there is a good chance that the camera picked up everything. When I installed them I made sure they were top of the range and able to pick up sound from twenty metres away so fingers crossed it worked properly. We will also have him on camera entering the apartment, both from the outside and the inside. And the hospital and police took photos and documented every injury baby. Even if we didn't manage to get the confession, we have a lot of other things that we can press charges on. He's going away for a long time, I'm sure of it".

Sophie nodded, strong and sure. Before gently pushing to her knees and straddling my hips, which wasn't an easy feat when you can't use your arms.

"Hugh?" she whispered, leaning her head to one side, looking at me with a shy smile.

"Yes honey?".

"Will you ... will you m-make love to me?". She asked unsurely, as if expecting me to refuse her.

"Are you sure baby? You know we don't have to. We can wait, there's no rush". I placed my hands on her hips, giving her a reassuring squeeze.

"I'm sure Hugh. I don't want him to be the last m-man to have touched me. I need you to take his touch away, replace it with yours. Will you? Can you d-do that for me?". I looked into her eyes, glistening with unshed tears.

I sat up, tucking her hair behind her ears before taking her face in mine and bringing my lips to hers.

"I'll take it away baby", I whispered, kissing her softly on her plump lips before I carefully picked her up and manoeuvred her to her back on the bed beneath me. She moved her legs apart, making space for me to crawl between them. I stroked my hands up and down her legs before reaching underneath her t-shirt and lowered her panties down her legs. Leaning over her to kiss her perfect pouty lips, running my tongue along the seam. She opened for me, allowing me entry as I swept my tongue into her mouth, tangling it with hers.

"We're leaving your t-shirt on baby, I don't want to hurt your arms," my voice was deep and growly, filled with need.

She nodded, lifting her lips back up to mine.

"Take your clothes off Hugh, I need you".

I leaned back on my haunches and whipped my t-shirt over my head, before standing to unbutton my jeans, lowering them down my legs along with my boxer briefs, standing before Sophie completely naked.

My cock was hard and ready for her. Standing tall and curved up towards my stomach. I knelt back on the bed and crawled back between her gorgeous legs.

"Let's see if you're ready for me shall we honey?" Looking up at her for permission before swiping my thumb through her wetness. She let out a moan.

"You're dripping for me baby". I plunged one finger deep inside of her warmth, slowly retreating before bringing another finger inside to join the first. She moaned and writhed beneath me.

"Hugh, I need you", she moaned.

"I'm here baby". I leaned across her, reaching for my bedside table for a condom. She tentatively brought a hand to my forearm to stop me,

"I got an IUD at my last doctors appointment. I'd really like you to fuck me bare, I want to feel you, skin to skin. I want to feel you inside me. If you want to, of course?". She asked shyly, looking from one eye to the other, waiting for my reaction.

It was a no brainer obviously, I wanted to feel my woman bare more than anything. I wanted to fill her with my seed and then watch it seep back out of her all over my sheets.

I couldn't hold back the deep groan that left my chest,

"I want that too baby, more than anything. Are you sure?". I grabbed a hold of the base of my solid cock and pointed it towards her slick entrance.

She nodded.

"I need your words honey," I murmured.

"I'm sure Hughie, fuck me, fuck me bare". If she could have grabbed me and pulled me forward herself, I knew she would have done.

There was no need, I was there, I was ready and as I plunged into her tight wet heat I saw stars.

"Fuck baby, you're so tight," I groaned.

Sophie pulled her feet up against my arse and pulled me deeper inside of her, moaning out loud in pure ecstasy.

"Ah yeah, fuck you feel good. Fuck me Hugh, fuck me hard".

I couldn't hold back any more, I slowly withdrew right to the tip before pounding back inside of her, hard.

I was frantic, pounding into her body as hard as I could, pushing her up the bed towards to the headboard. Which I grabbed a hold of for leverage, I wanted to grab Sophie and pull her harder onto my cock but I wouldn't hurt her more.

She moaned beneath me, uttering unintelligible nonsense. I couldn't make out a word, which made me huff a small laugh and lower my chin to my chest as I continued to pound her into the mattress.

She began to tighten around me, her inner muscles quivering with her impending orgasm. I wasn't far behind her. She felt divine. We fit together perfectly, "You're taking me so well baby".

I slammed my lips to hers, muttering against her swollen lips,

"Come for me honey, come all over my cock".

She exploded, her body went stiff and she shook beneath me, moaning my name.

"Hugh ..... yes yes yes". Her pussy gripped me hard, pulling me deeper into her body. The tingling started in my spine, creeping up into my balls as I shot my load deep inside of her. Streaming pulse after pulse of hot come into her channel, coating her inner walls with a deep, long groan.

It seemed to go on forever and when I finally slumped down onto Sophie's chest and she tried her best to hold me close, everything finally felt right in the world. We were safe and we were together.

# Chapter Twenty-Nine

## Sophie

It had been a week since I'd lived through hell and come out the other side. Physically I was still sore, my shoulders felt bruised and beaten and my wrists were itchy and red. I was beginning to heal though, for which I was incredibly grateful. The entire experience could have turned out a completely different way and I couldn't even begin to bring myself to consider the alternatives.

I'd spent a week living with Hugh and Lucie and it had been so nice. Hugh was so loving and comforting, he held me through my tears, backed me up when I was feeling angry and built me back up emotionally and physically.

I was feeling much stronger than I had done just a few days ago, it was time to get back home and start living again. I wasn't going to let Liam push me out of my home.

I'd truly loved staying at Hugh's and if I'm being honest, I'd stay here forever. Both Hugh and Lucie made my heart feel full and I didn't want to leave. One day if our relationship progressed then maybe I would move in here for real. That was what I was hoping for, but I didn't want it to be because something awful had happened to me. I wanted it to be because that's what we both wanted.

Hugh was attentive and amazing but I saw the struggles that he tried to keep locked up inside, he felt guilty for feeling happy. He felt sad that he believed he was letting Grace down. I could understand and I definitely empathised. I wasn't going to rush him into anything he wasn't ready for. This would happen when it was supposed to happen, *if* it was supposed to happen.

I may not be ready to share my feelings with Hugh, but I could admit to myself that I was completely and utterly, head over heels in love with him and not just because I felt as if he'd saved me.

Hugh was an unbelievable man. He was kind, attentive, loving, smart, honest and incredibly loyal. Add to the fact that the guy was unbelievably handsome and had a hard, muscled tattooed body I just wanted to run my tongue over. He was sweet and generous and undeniably dominant in the bedroom. The man was perfect and I couldn't get enough of him.

His daughter was pretty incredible too. Lucie was such an adorable girl, she was sweet and funny and had the biggest heart. I'd be incredibly honoured to be a bigger part of her life. Of course, I'd never replace her mother and I'd never want to. But, I think I could be a pretty good best friend to that little girl.

But for now, it was time for me to go home. I wasn't frightened. It wasn't the place that had hurt me, it was Liam. As I opened up my front door, I was completely assaulted with the stench of pine and bleach. Hugh mentioned that Ace and Lily had been by and cleaned up for me. What he didn't mention was that they had completely rearranged every piece of furniture, cleaned down every surface and even placed a fresh bunch of tulips on the kitchen side. I smiled to myself as I noticed a small handwritten note placed on the counter beside them.

---

*We had a little move around and freshen up. It's a brand new place now, fit for a warrior. Check your wardrobe, Hugh has left you a little something. See you tonight, A + L x*

---

163

Tonight was New Years Eve and I was ready to let my hair down. Hugh's parents were looking after Lucie so we had the whole night to ourselves. I couldn't wait to have a few drinks and some fun with our friends, my new family.

I placed the note back on the counter and took off towards my bedroom in search of my present from Hugh. Before I opened my bedroom door, I paused, taking a deep breath before entering. Hugh had offered to come inside with me but I'd told him that it was something I needed to do alone, I refused to be afraid of my own home. I could do this. So with that thought filling my mind, I opened the bedroom door ...

I hardly recognised the place. In place of my tiny double bed was a huge, luxurious super king size bed. It was covered in beautiful violet bedding with a pristine white sheet. The headboard was wooden, with intricately carved flowers decorating it. It was stunning. Copious amounts of purple, grey and white scatter pillows were artfully placed across the pillows and one single red rose lay across the middle. God if I wasn't already in love with that man, this would have secured it.

My bedroom furniture had been rearranged too, it looked like a brand new room. There was not a speck of evidence left from what had happened to me and for that I was relieved.

I headed to the wardrobe, finding a white dress bag hanging front and centre. I gingerly grabbed the hanger and lowered it down on the bed, my shoulders were still aching, stretching and lifting were still difficult.

I slowly lowered the zip and let out a small gasp when I found the most stunning dark red velvet dress. It was off the shoulder, a thin belt around the middle to cinch in at the waist and it looked to be around knee length. It was beautiful, stunning, gorgeous. I was going to feel like a million bucks in this.

Also inside the wardrobe was a white box, wrapped in gold and red ribbon. It held the most stunning golden heels and also a thin pair of golden slippers. I couldn't help but bark out a laugh when I saw them, Hugh was beginning to know me well. I couldn't last more than an hour in a pair of heels, the slippers would definitely be needed. They'd also fit perfectly in the matching golden purse which was also in the box.

My heart thumped in my chest as tears burned the back of my eyes. Nobody had ever thought about my needs so thoroughly before. Hugh had thought of everything. As I reached for the purse, I noticed it had something inside. I undid the popper to find a small box inside, a velvet box. Opening it up to discover the most beautiful gold star shaped earrings, with small hanging diamonds. With a matching necklace with the world 'Honey' engraved within the star.

Hugh may never be able to tell me how he feels, but I could feel it. I felt his love and I saw in his actions how much he cared for me.

My phone buzzed in the back pocket of my jeans, I reached for it.

**Hugh: You ok in there baby? x**

My heart fluttered in my chest and butterflies burst to life inside my belly.

**Me: I'm fine Hughie. I've just opened your present. Has anybody ever told you how unbelievably perfect you are?! Thank you so much for everything. Not just my gifts, but everything x**

**Hugh: Worth every single penny honey. You ok being in there? x**

**Me: I'm ok, I promise. It wasn't as hard as I thought it was going to be. It helps that it doesn't even look like my apartment. I can't thank you all enough x**

**Hugh: You mean a lot to us all Sophie. You have us all for life. I'll see you in about two hours ok, I can't wait to see you in that dress. And take you out of it later on! x**

**Me: Mmm I'll look forward to that VERY much Mr Weston. I'll see you soon and thank you again for all of my gifts x**

I threw my phone onto my bed as I heard a rumble come from outside. I ran to the window just in time to see Hugh's truck driving past. He hung his hand outside the window, waving goodbye as he cruised past down the road with a smile plastered across his face.

He had waited for me. He had stayed outside to make sure I was alright before driving away.

Geez, I was crazy about that man!

We danced, we laughed and we chatted for hours. We were at Mack and Maisie's three bedroom house in the village celebrating New Years. It was just the eight of us, Myself and Hugh, Freya and Ryan, Lily and Ace and of course Maisie and Mack.

I was on my third pina colada and was starting to loosen up. I hadn't laughed this much in such a long time. My stomach hurt. The 90's tunes were banging and us girls were stumbling all over the place, well, not me, I'd changed into my slippers an hour ago.

I'd just finished bumping and grinding with Maisie when I excused myself to use the bathroom. I climbed the stairs one by one, holding tightly to the hand rail. I wasn't drunk, just a little buzzed. Next thing I knew, a pair of warm hands descended on my arse and a hard chest pressed against my back.. The scent of pure man and whiskey assaulted my senses and I couldn't stop my body from pushing back into his. He pushed me forward by my hips, leading me towards the only bathroom in the house.

"What are you up to Mr Weston?" I asked flirtatiously.

"Hmm … just needed a little …breather," he hummed.

"Oh is that right? And what does this 'breather' entail?"

"Well it entails me getting on my knees and finding out if you're wearing panties underneath this gorgeous dress," he whispered into my ear, sending shivers skating down my spine.

"Mm hm". When the bathroom door was closed and locked behind us, I placed a palm on the top of Hugh's head, grabbing a handful of his soft brown locks and began pushing him down onto his knees.

He gave me a smirk and went willingly, slowing on his journey to press kisses to my neck, down the valley between my breasts before finally taking to his knees in front of me. His warm hands caressed my ankles, up my calves and the back of my thighs before landing on my bare arse. He let out a deep groan,

"Fucking hell honey. You've been strutting your stuff down there, grinding all over me and now I find out that this sweet little pussy is bare for me … hmm … I need a taste". He threw a leg over his shoulder, hiking my dress up around my waist and planted those lips firmly between my legs. He then spent the next twenty minutes showing me exactly how delicious he thought I was. Before I got to my knees, taking him in my mouth until his eyes rolled into the back of his head and he shuddered down my throat.

We eventually stumbled back out of the bathroom, barely able to keep our hands off of each other. We abruptly stopped when the door to the spare bedroom flew open to our right and Ace came flying out. He was furious, he looked like he was ready to tear the place apart.

"Fuck this and fuck you! How the fuck could you?". He shouted and pointed a finger back towards Lily who stood inside the bedroom with her face in her hands and her shoulders shaking.

"Oh shit," Hugh said under his breath. With a quick kiss pressed to my cheek and a silent nod. Hugh ran off down the stairs after a furious Ace, as I moved towards Lily slowly, like I was approaching a wounded animal.

"Lily honey, what happened?" I took her in my arms and pulled her to me. I'd never seen Lily upset before, she was always the smiling bubbly one. But right now as I held her close, she sobbed violently into my neck. Barely able to take in a full breath.

"I fucked up Soph, I really fucked up".

She didn't tell me any more, I couldn't tell if she was embarrassed, ashamed or just didn't want to talk about it but after a little while, she straightened her shoulders and wiped away her tears. She took a few deep breaths before heading into the bathroom to freshen up, I hoped it didn't still smell like sex in there!

I waited outside when she finally re-emerged ten minutes later, completely put together.

"Come on, I don't want to ruin anyone else's night". She took me by the hand and led me back down the stairs. Hugh was waiting for me at the bottom with a worried look on his face, I looked at him asking the silent question if Ace was ok. He gave me a slow shake of his head,

"He left," he whispered in my ear when I was close enough for him to sweep me back into his arms.

"Do you know what happened?" he asked. I gave him a shake of my head before we followed Lily back into the living room. Just in time for the countdown to midnight. She headed straight for the kitchen and the half full bottle of vodka on the counter as the rest of us counted down …

"10, 9, 8, 7, 6, 5, 4, 3, 2, 1 ... Happy New Year!". Maisie, Mack, Freya and Ryan seemed to be completely oblivious to what had just happened, so we went along with the façade.

Hugh took me in his arms and kissed the ever loving shit out of me as we saw in our first New Years together. He placed his hands on my shoulders and turned me around just in time to see Ryan lower to one knee in front of a completely shocked Freya, her eyes flicked around the room in surprise before settling back on her man in front of her.

"Freya, you are my everything. You are my best friend, my soul mate, my light, my love. You bring me more joy than I could have ever hoped for. I love you Fifi. Will you make me the happiest man in the whole world and be my wife? Will you marry me?". Ryan's voice was shaking, his hands trembling as he held up the most beautiful diamond ring in front of Freya.

Tears streamed down her face, as she took to her knees in front of him, took his face between her hands and whispered "Yes, yes, yes," before taking his lips with hers.

Tears were flowing down my cheeks with happiness for her. She was so deserving of a happy ending, especially after everything she had been through with losing her little sister.

I looked over my shoulder and took in Hugh's red rimmed eyes as a silent tear trickled down his cheek and a slow smile spread across his face. Freya was like a sister to him, they were incredibly close. I knew it meant the world to him that she was happy.

Well this had been one hell of a New Years, one I wouldn't forget in a while. Hugh and I had done very dirty things to each other in someone else's bathroom. Lily and Ace had potentially broken up after a huge screaming match. Ace had disappeared and Lily was currently slumped up against the back door gulping neat vodka from the bottle and Freya and Ryan were engaged. The only couple who were behaving remotely like their normal selves was Maisie and Mack. Mack who was sitting comfortably on his brown leather sofa, currently enjoying a less that private, very graphic lap dance from his beautiful wife, who was incredibly drunk and flashing body parts that she was entirely unaware of.

What a night to remember.

## Hugh

The next few weeks flew by with a mix of work at the fire station, spending time with Lucie and Sophie, dance class, pre-school and spending time with our friends and my folks.

Before I knew it, it was the beginning of February and it was edging closer to the three year anniversary of Grace's death. This year was going to be a different one. I still missed Grace with every fibre of my being, I always would. She was the very first love of my life.

But meeting Sophie and getting to know her was healing me, mending me deep inside and making life a little easier to bear. I couldn't help but feel guilty for that though. I hoped that maybe one day I'd find someone special to care about again but I never envisioned that it would be only three years since Grace had died.

I felt like I was betraying her, like I was tainting my own memory of her and that brought a heaviness to my heart that I wasn't quite sure how to handle.

I'd always love Grace and I'd always miss her. And more importantly I'd always make sure that Lucie knew where she came from and that her mother loved her more than anything else in the world.

Every amazing day I spend with Sophie, just made me feel more guilty. It was crippling me. We would spend hours laughing, talking, cuddling and making love and in the moment it felt truly incredible. Like this was where I was always supposed to be. She made my chest clench, butterflies fluttered in my tummy and just the mere thought of seeing her and holding her was enough to bring me to my knees.

It was when she went home and I was left alone with my thoughts that my mind was tangled. I couldn't comprehend how something so incredible that felt so right, could feel so wrong at the same time.

I wasn't oblivious, I knew my feelings were growing for her. If I dug really deep then I could admit to myself that I was falling in love with her and I was pretty sure that she felt the same way. She was so patient with me, so careful and loving. I think she knew that I was struggling. She never pressured me, she never made me feel as though I had to say or do certain things to keep her around. Although, I knew that would only last for so long, she wouldn't stick around long term if I wasn't able to open up and commit to her fully.

I hadn't written to Grace in a long while. I didn't know what I was supposed to say. She sure as hell wouldn't want to hear about her husband falling in love with someone else and envisioning a life with her, maybe marriage, maybe more kids in the future. I couldn't tell her that, I couldn't betray her like that. I made my vows to Grace, I couldn't break them even further than I already had. Could I?

I tried to keep myself busy, tried not to dwell on it too much. Maybe if I just ignored these conflicting feelings then they would just go away. The universe would sort it all out by itself and maybe my guilt would dwindle.

The closer we got to Grace's anniversary, the more I felt as if D-Day was approaching. I couldn't hold back forever and I definitely couldn't walk away. I was in too deep, Sophie made me feel things that I hadn't felt in a very long time. She was incredibly special and so god-damn addictive, I'd never get my fill of her.

I was saved from my spiralling by Lucie flying through the kitchen door and flinging herself down on a dining room chair, tightly clutching a packet of crayons and a folder full of papers.

"What're you up to Lucie Lu?" I asked as I went to join her at the table, pulling out a chair and sitting down, placing my cup of coffee in front of me.

"I'm making Mummy a special picture, Auntie Fifi said that it's almost Mummy's special day so I wanted to make her a special letter and picture". Lucie's speech had progressed so much over the past couple of months, she was no longer missing letters or getting phrases wrong. She was beginning to speak like a big kid, I wasn't sure how I felt about that.

"I think that's a lovely idea, can I make one too?".

"Sure," she said, sliding me a piece of paper and some crayons.

"What are you going to write in your letter?" I asked her. We had always spoken very openly about Grace, I wanted her to know who her Mum was.

"Well ... first of all I'm going to tell her how much I love her and miss her. Then I'm going to tell her all about dancing and school. Then I'm going to tell her about my day with Auntie Fifi I had the other day. And then ...". She hesitated, biting one of her tiny little finger nails.

"What is it Lu?" I asked.

"I um, I wanted to ask her if it's ok if I can love Sophie. I know that Sophie isn't my Mummy, but I'd really like to keep Sophie as my next Mummy. Do you think that would be ok?". She looked up at me with her huge brown eyes, full of hesitation and uncertainty. I was instantly stumped, not knowing how to respond, especially when minutes before I was dealing with my own internal conflict.

"You really love Sophie?".

Her eyes lit up, a smile spreading across her face.

"Oh yeah, I do. I love Sophie big. She's so funny and she always makes me laugh and she gives me the best snuggles. She always reads me those special stories she has in her bag. Did you know she has like twenty hundred special stories in there? She said that some of them are for grown ups so I can't read those ones but I'm allowed to read the kid ones and I really like them. She said that maybe one day I can have them on my bookshelf".

A lump formed in my throat, tears burned the back of my eyes as I took a deep swallow and tried to clear my throat. I knew that Sophie and Lucie got along great, they were the best of friends. I had no idea that Sophie had been sharing her writing with Lucie. I'd be sure to ask her about them, she was insanely talented.

It was inevitable that Lucie would fall in love with Sophie too right? Kids were free with their feelings, there were no strings attached. I couldn't tell Lucie how she was supposed to feel and I couldn't project my feelings onto her. I took a deep breath before telling her,

"I think you have a huge heart Lulu and I'm incredibly proud of you for that. You're kind and generous and we are all so lucky to have you. You've got a big family who loves you very much, we love you big. Auntie Fifi and Uncle Ryan, Auntie Maisie and Uncle Mack. Uncle Ace ... and Auntie Lily. Nana and Pop. They all love you so big baby. I also know that Sophie loves you too, she's a really special friend isn't she. But, do you know who loves you the biggest of all?".

She thought about it for a moment, before lifting those big eyes back to mine,

"You do Daddy, you love me the mostest. And my Mummy loves me, she isn't here with me any more but she loves me the mostest. Sometimes I wish she was here Daddy. All my friends at school have got Mummy's. I wish I had one too". Her big eyes filled with tears which began to trickle down her cheeks.

I was off my chair in an instant and scooped her into my arms as she sobbed into my chest.

"All the other Mummy's do my friends hairs, and they go out and do special things that only Mummy's do. I wish my Mummy was here". She whispered the last sentence and that was my undoing. I buried my face into Lucie's hair and let my tears fall. Maybe Lucie had been feeling as conflicted as I had. I knew the time would eventually come when Lucie began to really feel the absence of her Mum. She was getting older and beginning to notice what her friends had that she didn't.

"Your Mummy wishes she was here too baby. You were all she ever wanted, did you know that? All she ever wanted was to be your Mummy and she would do anything to be here if she could. Mummy got very sick and the doctors weren't able to save her, they tried, they really did. But Mummy just wasn't strong enough to stay. But even though she's not here with us, she would want you to be happy Lulu. You have her big heart and you love really big, just like she did. She would want you to love whoever you wanted to, so if you want to love Sophie then that's ok with me. I know it would be ok with Mummy too ok". I sniffed and wiped my tears on the back of my hand as Lucie nodded against my chest.

"Daddy?"

"Yes baby?"

"You have a big heart like me and Mummy, you love big too and you give the bestest snuggles. Do you think that Mummy would be ok with you loving Sophie too?".

All the breath left my lungs in an instant and the pain almost crippled me from the inside.

"I hope so baby," I managed to choke out.

"I really hope so". We stayed like that for a long while, holding each other tightly, missing and loving her Mummy before we went back to our letters and drawings ready to deliver to Grace's grave in a few days time.

# Chapter Thirty-One

## Sophie

It had been six weeks since that dreadful day with Liam. Physically I felt completely healed, everything felt like it was supposed to and I was no longer in any pain.

I'd been in touch with the police multiple times, who had some follow up questions. I'd passed on all of the evidence I'd managed to collect, which thankfully included very detailed CCTV photos, videos and audio from that dreadful night. My lawyer had also compiled all of the texts that Liam had been sending me relentlessly, my medical records and a written statement from my doctor detailing his findings. Along with statements from Hugh, Ace and Lily detailing what they walked into that day.

The day had finally come when Liam was going to court for sentencing, my lawyer felt very strongly that we had enough to convict him and that I could finally get him out of my life and move on.

I walked into that court room with my head held high. Hugh was beside me, his hand clasped firmly in mine, he hadn't left my side all morning. Maisie, Mack, Freya, Ryan, Ace and Lily all trailed in behind me. I'd never felt so loved and so relieved to have all of these people in my corner. Their support was unwavering. Although Ace and Lily were still not talking, they had definitely broken up and couldn't even bare to look at each other. We still didn't know what had happened between them. They were keeping that information locked up tight. But I was beyond grateful that they were able to put that to the side today and be here to support me.

We sat through hours of talking, arguing and evidence being shown and scrutinised. Apparently, Liam had pleaded guilty on all counts which surprised me massively. Never did I think he would go down without a fight but just looking at him across the courtroom, I could see that this man was not the man I married. He was broken, no life was left in his eyes. His eyes were bloodshot and red rimmed, his cheeks sunken in, his hair long and dishevelled. I couldn't help but feel a little bit of empathy for him, before me was a man that was truly broken. I'd loved this man not too long ago, I was woman enough to admit that I was hurting for him a little.

He had done unspeakable things to me, things that he could never take back. I knew deep within my heart that he was hurting, I knew he regretted every single thing that had happened and he would take them all back if he could. But, unfortunately he couldn't. He had made those decisions and carried out those actions. He had to be punished for them.

He never looked up from his lap, never gave me eye contact or gave any outward reaction to what was happening. Not until he was sentenced to fifteen years in prison with the chance of parole after ten. He was sentenced with harassment, drugging, breaking and entering with the intent to cause harm, attempted rape, false imprisonment, ABH and possession of a Class A drug.

Only then did his chest heave and tears fell down his cheeks, he sobbed into his hands, the sound of his heartbreak filling the room. Tears streamed down my cheeks too, not in relief, but in pain. Of course I hated what he had put me through but more than anything I hated the pain he was feeling. I had always prided myself on being a kind and compassionate person and I was able to feel those things for him. He made some terrible mistakes, I knew that and so did he.

As Liam stood up and was led out of the room, he stopped just inside the door. Turned around and looked right at me. He had heartbreak in his eyes, soul deep pain radiating from him as he mouthed "I'm so sorry Soph, I love you". He turned and was quickly led out of the room.

That's when I broke down. I cried for what I'd been through and I cried for what I'd survived. I cried in relief that it was over but most of all I cried for my husband.

For half of my life that man had been my best friend, my love and my safety net. The pain was deep, it filled my body to breaking point as I cried for the man I'd once loved with my whole heart. He wasn't him any more but I cried for who he had once been.

Hugh held me in his arms as I cried for another man, he rubbed my back and kissed my forehead as I spilled heartbroken tears into his white shirt.

Everybody else quietly excused themselves, giving Hugh and I a second to gather ourselves before we stood and got ready to leave. Hugh led me towards the exit before we were stopped by Liam's lawyer Chris. Who just so happened to be his friend and work colleague.

"Sophie!" he called.

I turned, still clutching Hugh's hand tightly.

Chris jogged down the aisle, holding a large brown envelope.

"I have something for you," he said as he held out the envelope to me, the other hand reaching to squeeze the top of my arm.

"I'm sorry for everything you've been through Sophie and I wish you the very best for the future". Short and sweet, he turned around a strode back down towards the judge.

It wasn't until hours later when I was tucked up in bed with a large glass of wine that I worked up the courage to open the envelope from Chris. I slid my finger along the seam and pulled out a stack of papers.

At the very top were signed divorce papers. Liam had signed them finally. He was finally letting me go, my eyes burned with unshed tears as I closed them and held the papers to my chest.

Second in the stack was the deed to our house, it was worth 1.4 million and here it was, all in my name. Liam has signed it all over the me, the house, the land, the cars, the holiday homes. The tears began to trickle down my face then, he'd given me everything. I didn't want anything from him, yet he'd given me everything.

The final paper in the stack caused my heart to stop as I sucked in a breath. It was a handwritten letter from Liam. The tears were streaming, my chest was heaving and my heart was pounding as I read his words.

---

**Dear Sophie,**
**There's nothing I can say to you to take back all the pain I've caused you over the years, but if I could, please believe me when I say I would.**
**I have no excuses for what I've put you through but please believe me when I tell you that none of it was your fault. I got lost. I got caught up in some terrible things that I couldn't get out of and instead of leaning on you and asking for your help, I sabotaged it all.**
**I am deeply ashamed of my recent behaviour, you know that's not me. I'd never want to hurt a hair on your head. You are the love of my life Sophie and I would do anything to change the outcome. I am so deeply sorry for everything I've done and I deserve whatever sentence I get. I won't fight it.**
**I deeply regret causing you pain and I'm incredibly sorry for not giving you the life you dreamed of and deserved.**

---

I'll work hard to get better, I'll make you proud and I'll work to become the man I wished I could have been for you.
I wish you all the happiness in the world Sophie, I know it's not with me and that's ok.
Be happy, fall in love and make lots of babies. You deserve the world. I pray that one day you can forgive me.
I'll love you always,
Liam x

I cried myself to sleep that night, holding tightly to Liam's letter. I fell asleep with forgiveness in my heart for the man who had once been the love of my life.

# Chapter Thirty-Two

## Sophie

It had been a long time since I'd been in a graveyard. Both of my parents were buried in a beautiful little graveyard in Norfolk. I didn't get to visit as much as I'd like to.

I was currently sat in the car watching Hugh and Lucie sitting in front of Grace's grave. Both with their arms laden with flowers, letters, cards and gifts. It had been three years since Grace had died, I couldn't even begin to comprehend how Hugh was feeling today. He had been quiet for the last couple of weeks, struggling with his inner turmoil, feeling guilty for moving on.

I'd spoken with Freya about it at great length and she assured me that I was doing the right thing. I didn't want to add any additional pressure to Hugh, he was already hurting enough. I told him that I was happy to stay at home today and give him and Lucie some privacy, but he assured me that I was welcome to come.

I sat in the car for a long time, the flowers and letter burning a hole in my handbag. I'd kept them hidden from Hugh, I wasn't entirely sure why. I hadn't even decided if I'd go through with it yet.

When Hugh and Lucie finally came back to the car, eyes red rimmed and tear stains streaking their cheeks, I took them both in my arms and held them tightly.

"I'll be back in a minute, ok?" I whispered into Hugh's ear, kissing them both on the forehead. He looked up at me with a half shocked, half in awe expression. He gave me a small nod before turning to buckle Lucie into her car seat.

I grabbed my bag and began to walk slowly towards Grace's grave. I didn't want to intrude or over step. Which is why I'd approached Freya beforehand. She assured me that Grace would love to meet me, she was always apparently so adamant that she wanted Hugh to find love again one day.

I stood in front of Grace's beautiful grave, it was laden with flowers and photos. There was a beautiful box in front of her gravestone which held letters and pictures. I felt eyes on me, caressing me from head to toe. I turned to find Hugh leaning against the front of his car, watching me with a curious expression.

I sat carefully in front of Grace and placed my hand on the photo of her on the gravestone. She was beautiful, a tiny brunette with the most gorgeous big brown eyes. She looked just like Lucie.

"Hi Grace". I spoke softly, I didn't know if she could hear me but I'd like to think so.

"I'm Sophie, I'm sure you've seen me around". I lowered my hand, resting them both in my lap. Holding onto the white daisy bouquet and handwritten letter.

"I wanted to read you something if that's ok?", as I laid the daisies down on the soft green grass.

"I've written you a letter. I've been spending a little time with Freya and she told me that you'd want to meet me someday. So here I am, if you want me to bugger off now is your chance to tell me". I said with a smile, looking up into the sky, waiting to be struck by lightning or something. I waited a few seconds before looking back towards Grace.

"Ok, I'll take that as a sign to carry on," I huffed a small laugh before unfolding my letter and lowering my eyes to read.

To Grace,

First of all I'd like to say that I'm so incredibly sorry to hear about what happened to you. I can't even begin to imagine the fear and the pain you must have gone through. Not just physically, but deep inside your heart too. Both Hugh and Freya have told me how unbelievably brave and strong you were and how you'd found peace in your diagnosis in the end.

I am in awe of you Grace, you were a warrior.

Now, I'm guessing you've been watching the past couple of months and thinking what the hell is that little woman doing with your family. I felt I should come and explain myself.

I've spent my whole life feeling pretty alone, even when I was surrounded by people. I went through some stuff and ended up here and I've never felt more at home in my life.

I've fallen undeniably in love with your daughter, she is incredible. The kindest, purest, most generous and beautiful little soul. She looks just like you and you should be so proud.

So, now is the hard part and Freya insists that I should tell you. I've fallen head over heels, totally and completely in love with Hugh. He is a very special man. He is kind and sweet, generous and beyond handsome as you know well yourself.

He's hurting Grace, he feels like he's betraying you. I know you wanted him to find love, for himself and for Lucie. He just needs a little sign that it's ok.

Ok, so enough waffling. I never got the pleasure of meeting you, but I feel like you're a long lost friend and I would like to think that we would have gotten along well.

I want to make you some promises before I go.

> **I promise to love them both with my whole heart. I promise to keep them safe and hold their hands when they are feeling lost and scared.**
> **I promise to love them completely and unconditionally.**
> **I promise to spend the rest of my life loving your family just as fiercely as you do, if you'll let me.**
> **It was lovely to finally meet you Grace, I'll come back and keep you updated on life soon.**
> **Love Sophie x**

Silent tears streamed down my cheeks as I finished my letter and posted it in the little post box that was already pretty full to the brim.

I climbed to my feet and laid a hand on the top of Grace's gravestone, ready to say goodbye for now.

At that very moment, a stunning white and pink butterfly fluttered down from the skies and landed directly on the back of my hand. I stood wide eyed and frozen, not daring to move an inch. The butterfly stood on my hand for a full minute before turning and taking off back towards the sky.

I felt free from guilt, I'd been carrying my own around for the past few months. My tears were cathartic and I felt ready to move on. I felt like Grace had given me her blessing. I know lots of people don't believe in receiving messages from beyond the grave, but I felt deep in my heart that Grace was ok. Not just at peace, but ok with me loving her family.

It was around a week later when Hugh and I had taken Lucie out for a picnic in the middle of Meadowside Woodland Park. Like its namesake, Meadowside featured the most beautiful meadow which seemed to go on for miles. There was long grass seeded with wildflowers. Bees, dragonflies and butterflies buzzed and fluttered around our heads. Tall trees budding with new leaves surrounded us. Birds sang in the skies. Mushrooms, wild strawberry plants and insects popping up from the ground. Sunlight bursts through the trees, lightening up the rainbow of flowers surrounding us. It truly was a beautiful place at the beginning of Spring. We spent hours laughing, reading stories and drawing pictures. Hugh had asked me about my writing and I'd told him about my dreams to become a successful author. I told him about my vision of owning a little bakery slash bookshop, which I'd originally planned to call 'Lost and Found'. I had different plans now. I kept that little detail to myself for now though. He thought it was an amazing idea and now that I was apparently loaded thanks to Liam, I could perhaps afford to finally do it. Maybe.

Lucie was off exploring the trees not far from us, catching insects in her little fruit pot from lunch. Hugh and I were laid on the red and white chequered picnic blanket staring up at the sky, watching the birds fly in circles above our heads. Hugh held me in his arms, my head laid on his chest while he twirled my brown curls around his finger.

He had seemed a little more at peace since the anniversary of Grace's death had passed. He never did ask me what I spoke about with Grace at her grave that day. He just looked at me with awe in his eyes, held me close and wiped away my tears with his thumbs.

We lay for a long time in each other's arms, listening to Lucie talking to the bugs and birds, trapped in our own thoughts.

My heart began to race as I contemplated what was in my heart, what I was ready to let out into the world. I didn't want to scare him away, but I couldn't hold it in any more. I was beyond scared about his reaction, whether he would run and push me away or whether he would feel it and say it back. I believed I was more likely to get the first reaction but secretly prayed for the second. My heart was guarded, I knew this moment probably wasn't going to be like in the movies and romance books. But I needed to say it, I needed to set it free and let it fly. I took a deep breath, closed my eyes and prayed for strength.

"Hugh?" I whispered, my voice wobbling with nerves.

"Hmm?" he asked, his arms were closed and he had a small smile on his face. He looked so peaceful I almost felt bad that I was most likely about to send him into a spiral of turmoil.

"I love you Hugh. I'm completely, totally, unconditionally in love with both you and Lucie. I didn't know how lonely I was until I met you, you've taken my pain away, you're my missing piece. I love you". I blurted out before blowing out a breath and closing my eyes, waiting for the blow of heartbreak to hit me.

His body stiffened beneath mine, his chest heaving against my cheek. I peeked up through my lashes to look at his face, he looked in pain. His eyes screwed up tightly and his mouth set in a firm line.

I waited and waited.

He didn't say a word, gave no inclination of his thoughts. He still held me close, his finger frozen in my hair but he didn't utter a single word.

We lay for a long time, going back to staring up at the sky. Before we knew it, the sun was beginning to set and it was time to go home. We packed up in silence, each only talking to Lucie when she asked questions. We packed up the truck and headed home.

Hugh dropped me off at my apartment, getting out of the car to walk me up the stairs to say goodnight, just like always.

He pulled me into his arms at the top of the stairs, held me tightly and kissed me gently on the forehead before turning away and walking back towards the truck.

He opened the door, started the engine and pulled away. Lucie's little hand waving at me through the window.

I let myself inside and just stood there in the entryway. What the hell had just happened? And why did that kiss just feel like goodbye?

# Chapter Thirty-Three

**Hugh**

*Dear Sweetheart,*
*I'm sorry. Sophie told me that she loved me a few days ago and*
*I'm pretty sure that I love her too.*
*I'm so sorry,*
*Love Hugh x*

It had been three days since Sophie had opened up her heart to me and told me that she loved me. She was so brave and honest, I know that must have been hard for her, she was so in tune with how I was feeling, she must have known that it was a risk telling me.

I didn't want it to be a risk and I didn't want her to feel like she couldn't be open and honest with me. I'd do anything to rewind back to that moment and change the way I reacted.

Even if I hadn't felt ready to say it back, I should have said something! I completely shut down and didn't utter a single word. What a selfish bastard, an utter coward. I knew this but I just could not get past the fact that I was letting Grace down. She had died three years ago, only three years. It didn't seem like long enough to have moved on and fallen in love again.

But, I had. I mean how could I not have. Sophie was perfect and so god-damn lovable it was laughable. She was sweet and sexy, kind, loving, generous, understanding and so loyal. She not only loved me but she said she had fallen in love with Lucie too.

I felt like an utter bastard for not saying it back. The way she looked into my eyes when I said goodbye to her on the steps, the complete heartbreak I saw there. I couldn't take that back and I had no idea how to make it better.

I knew that I was in love with her too, completely and deeply. I'd known for a while now but I'd been too scared to admit it, to myself or to her. Now I felt like I'd lost her. I hadn't spoken to her in three days, she hadn't text me and I hadn't text her either. We couldn't be over though could we?

I couldn't give up on this second chance, she was incredible and so damn perfect for me and Lucie. How could I get past this guilt? I knew that there was only one person who I could talk to that would be able to talk me down and give me the reassurance I needed. Unfortunately that person wasn't here any more.

But, I still found myself sitting in front of Grace's grave on a rainy Wednesday afternoon. I'd finished work and driven straight here. I could barely concentrate at work, let alone hold a conversation with the guys.

Ace still wasn't back to his usual self, he seemed quiet and always stuck deep in his own thoughts. I couldn't put this on him too.

I sat in silence with Grace for a little while before finally building up the confidence to say what I needed to.

"Gracie, you know I love you with all my heart don't you? You were my very first true love, Lucie was my second. I miss you every single second of every single day. I'd do anything to be able to talk to you right now, I need your help. You own my heart and you always will, but ... Sophie does too". My voice cracked as the first tear fell.

"I think I've loved her since the very first moment I laid eyes on her, she's sweet and beautiful and so amazing with Lucie. I know you're watching us from up there in heaven, I still feel you with me everyday". Sobs shook my shoulders as I struggled to catch my breath. Tears were streaking rivers down my cheeks, my chest hurt.

"I ...I love Sophie so much Grace, please be ok with that. I know you told me that you didn't want me to be alone forever. You told me that I was allowed to love again. I just want you to know that my love for Sophie doesn't take away my love for you. You'll always be in my heart, but ... you were my first true love, Lucie was my second and Sophie is my third. I'm so sorry Grace". The heartbreak I felt in that moment was profound. My grief comes in waves, gruelling, painful, stealing appetite and sleep alike. The agony never leaves and it never will, but the love that Sophie brings to my life dulls the edges. She makes it liveable, she's my missing piece as much as I'm hers.

I sat on that muddy grass crying my heart out, for the woman I'd already lost and the love that I hoped to chase. The rain mixed with my tears as I grappled with my feelings.

A warm hand landed on my shoulder which made me startle, I hadn't heard footsteps or felt a presence. I was too consumed with my heartbreak to notice someone approaching.

Freya stood above me, sheltered under a huge umbrella. Silent tears fell down her cheeks as she took a seat next to me on the grass and leaned her head against my shoulder. I had no idea how long she'd been standing there and how much she'd heard.

"You know she would be so proud of you right?" she asked softly.

"I'm not so sure about that Fifi," I sniffled, wiping my tears away with the back of my hand and attempting to catch my breath.

"She would, and I think it's time Hugh". A small smile graced her face as her tears continued to fall.

"Time for what?". My voice broke as I asked.

"Time for this ..." Freya reached into her jacket pocket and pulled out a crinkled envelope which had been folded in half. It looked old, like it had been written a long time ago.

Freya handed it to me with one hand, still tightly clutching the umbrella in the other. On the front of the envelope was my name, written in Grace's beautiful handwriting. My eyes whipped to Freya's, she held a sad smile on her face and gave me a solemn nod.

"I promised Grace to only give you this letter when I believed you were ready to hear it. It's time Hughie," she said again as she wrapped her free arm around me, holding me tight. The rain continued to pour around us, the raindrops pounding against the earth being the only sound to be heard.

I pulled open the letter, taking care not to rip the edges. I took it out and was instantly hit with a barricade of memories. I never thought I'd hear from Grace ever again, the fact that she had thought ahead was more than I ever knew I needed. I'd do anything to get just one moment back with her.

I brought the letter to my chest, closing my eyes and leaning my head back towards the sky.

"I love you Gracie," I whispered into the atmosphere.

I took one deep breath and then another and then lowered my wet eyes to read my wife's last words to me.

---

*Dear Hughie,*
*If you're reading this letter then it means that I've been gone for a while. For that I'm so sorry.*
*I'm sorry I left you when you and Lucie needed me the most, I would have stayed with you forever if I could have. You two are the absolute loves of my lives.*
*I miss you endlessly, but know that I'm ok. I'm at peace and I'm not in pain any more.*
*You're reading this letter now because my Fifi thinks you're ready. You've fallen in love again Hugh and I'm so*

*proud of you. My only wish for you was for you to forgive yourself and find love again.*

*You love big Hugh Weston and if I know you as well as I think I do then you'll be feeling pretty guilty right about now.*

*Don't, you don't need to feel guilty baby.*

*Love her, love big and love forever. If she is the one, then show her, tell her. Shout it from the rooftops.*

*My final wish for you is to be happy, be the happiest you can be and live your life the way you always wanted to.*

*I know you'll never stop loving me and I'll never stop loving you. You are my one true love but it's now time for you to have your next true love.*

*Give Lucie a huge hug from me baby and tell her that I'll love and miss her forever.*

*This next part is for your new lady ...*

*We never got to meet but I just wanted to say thank you. Thank you for loving our Hughie and dulling his pain and grief just a little bit.*

*Make sure he lives his life with no regrets ok. Get married, have babies and live happily ever after. And love my baby girl as if she's your own, she deserves to have a Mummy that can hold her every day, wipe away her tears when she's sad and celebrate her smiles when she's happy.*

*Don't let her forget me will you.*

*Hughie, it's time for me to say goodbye for now, live your life baby. Share that big heart with those who deserve it.*

*I'll see you again someday,*

*Love Always,*

*Your Grace x*

Freya and I sat at Grace's grave in silence for a long while, wiping away our tears and holding each other tightly. More than anything I had needed Grace's blessing and I never thought I'd get to have it, but that angel woman had thought of everything. She gave me the strength I needed to get up off of that muddy, wet grass. Brush myself down and go and find the woman I loved so I could tell her that I was ready. I was ready to be loved by her, ready to love her back, ready to move on.

# Chapter Thirty-Four

## Sophie

I had been slaving away in the kitchen at the café for hours, baking cakes, pastries, pies. You name it, I was baking it. For no other reason than ignoring the absolute train wreck of my love life.

It had been three long days since I'd told Hugh I loved him and three long days since I'd heard from him. No texts, no calls, no visits. Just complete radio silence.

I should feel bad for dumping my feelings all over him but I just couldn't. He deserved to know and I deserved to be able to share that with him.

The only regret I had was that I'd obviously hurt him, I'd pushed him away and my heart was breaking a little more each day that went by without me hearing from him.

So here I was, elbow deep in flour and sugar, baking to my hearts content, trying to escape my life. The customers would be pretty happy with today's options that was for sure. Trudie let me be, I'd broken down in tears on the first day and told her what had happened. Over the months since coming here, she had become somewhat of a confidante, she was the mother figure I'd been so desperately missing for such a long time.

She had held me while I cried and told me "Sweetie, sometimes the head takes a little longer to catch up with the heart. That man loves you, he just needs to give himself permission to feel it. Give him time".

So that's what I was doing, waiting and hoping like hell that he loved me too. If not now, then maybe he could someday. I'd take someday over nothing at all.

I was in the pantry, searching for more ingredients when I heard a bang, it was loud enough to make me jump. The fire alarm started blaring loudly shortly after. *What the hell?* I put down everything I was holding in my arms and rushed towards the pantry door, but as I got there somebody ran past in a panic and the pantry door was slammed shut in my face.

*Fuck!* I was stuck, the pantry door only opens from the outside which is why I'd used a can of beans to hold it open for a few minutes while I was inside. I pulled on the handle from the inside, although I knew it was pointless. It didn't open of course so I began slamming my fists into the wooden door and screaming for help,

"Trudie! Mitch! Someone help me, I'm stuck!". Nobody could hear me over the wailing of the fire alarm overhead. I didn't think much of it, the fire alarm was going off quite often, especially when Trudie was left in charge of the kitchen. Someone would soon wonder where I was and come looking for me, wouldn't they?

I took a seat on the floor and opened up a bag of raisins, might as well have a snack while I sit here and wait. The pantry was just off of the main hallway, between the kitchen and the bathrooms. Someone would come along this way soon, I just had to be patient. I sat on the floor, eating raisins and humming my favourite Lewis Capaldi song.

Five minutes went by, then ten and the fire alarm still hadn't gone off. Was it just me or was it getting hot in here? I shuffled over to the closed door and placed my hand on the wood, I'm pretty sure it was warmer than it had been a few minutes earlier.

My heart began to race, the panic slowly starting to creep in. Just as I lowered down onto my stomach, attempting to look under the crack of the door, a waft of smoke filled my face and immediately made me cough and my eyes burn.

Oh no no no no, there was a fire and I was stuck. In the pantry behind a closed door, in the very middle of the building. The fire alarm still wailing overhead, nobody would hear my screams even if I tried.

I backed away slowly from the door, pushing myself tightly into the corner of the pantry as the room began to fill with smoke. It was thick and black, it burnt my eyes and throat as I began to cough violently.

I looked around the room frantically searching for something to help me. I quickly grabbed a stack of tea towels from the shelf, throwing them to the floor behind me. There was nothing else in here apart from cupboards filled with food and baking ingredients.

The room was thick with smoke now as I held a tea towel tightly to my mouth and nose, desperately trying to keep the smoke out.

My lungs were beginning to hurt as I coughed so hard that I was retching. I kept searching for something to help, as if I could conjure up help if I prayed for it hard enough.

The cupboard. That was my only line of defence against the thick putrid smoke, I crawled on the hands and knees across the room and began pulling everything out of the waist height cupboard. Flour, sugar, cream of tartar. It all went flying across the floor as I pulled myself inside the cupboard and pulled the door shut behind me. At this moment in time I was incredibly grateful for being so short!

It didn't stop the smoke completely, but it did give me a very small reprieve whilst I tried to catch my breath.

My lungs hurt, my throat burned, my eyes were watering and felt as though I had fragments of glass behind my eyelids. The heat was scorching, beads of sweat trickled down my spine and fell from my forehead into my eyes.

*I was going to die.*

I didn't want to die, I wasn't ready. I needed to be loved by Hugh, by Lucie. I needed to build a new life and have babies. I needed to write my books and open up a bakery bookshop. I couldn't let Hugh lose someone else, he wouldn't survive it.

I fought with all my might to breath, the tea towel still firmly held to my mouth and nose.

The world was closing in on me, my lungs were struggling to find any oxygen and as the cupboard began to spin around me and the world began to turn black I only had one thought in my mind.

*I love you Hugh Weston. I love you Lucie. Please forgive me.*

# Hugh

I was a man on a mission, I flew down the road in my truck. Barely keeping within the speed limit as I headed straight towards Trudie's. I was pretty sure that Sophie would be working today and I couldn't wait a minute more to make things right.

As I crested the hill that would lead me down towards the village, a plume of smoke could be seen rising into the air in the distance. Wow, that looked like a big fire. I'd have to go and check it out and see if the guys needed any help.

It wasn't until I was a few minutes down the road that it suddenly hit me like a ton of bricks - the smoke that I see flurrying in the sky was in the exact direction that I was heading. I quickly lifted my phone out of my pocket to check for missed calls, I'd put my phone on silent whilst I was with Grace and had forgotten to turn it back on loud.

*10 missed calls* Shit! All from Trudie, that definitely wasn't a good sign. I pressed call, no answer. I tried again, still no answer. I pushed my foot down a little harder on the peddle, I couldn't get there quick enough.

Sirens began to blare behind me as I pulled onto the High Street. Two fire engines raced down the road past me and came to a halt outside Trudie's at the end of the road. That's when I saw it, flames were licking at the front of the building, deep black smoke lifting towards the sky.

I could hear the crackle from here and the heat of the fire hit me as soon as I stepped out of the truck. I didn't even close my truck door before I took off, sprinting as fast as I could towards Trudie and Mitch who were standing outside of the café. Mitch was holding a screaming Trudie in his arms, trying to pull her back as she fought to get back into the building.

A lead weight hit my stomach and I couldn't see past the tragedy that I was pretty sure was unfolding right before my eyes.

I stopped in front of Trudie, grabbing her shoulders tightly and turning her towards me.

"Where's Sophie?" I shouted, my voice cracked in my throat. This couldn't be happening, not again. I knew what she was going to say before the words even left her mouth.

"S-She was inside, she hasn't c-come out Hugh". The world as I knew it crashed to the floor, time stood still and the earth fell silent. The only sound was the buzzing in my ears and the thumping of my heart. I fell to my knees on the concrete.

The noise that left my throat was inhuman,

"Noooooo, no no no. I didn't get to tell her, I didn't get to tell her". I had to tell her, if it was the last thing I did she had to know that I loved her too.

I was on my feet again and running towards the fire engine in a flash, I could hear Ace calling my name but it seemed so far away. I couldn't hear him, I couldn't hear anything. All I knew is that I could not lose another love, I just couldn't do it. I had to find her.

I undressed right there in the middle of the High Street, not giving a fuck who could see me stood in my boxers in the middle of the village. I heaved myself into the back of the engine and found the spare equipment that we always kept inside. I heaved on my fire proof equipment, barely giving myself time to slide the helmet over my head before I was running.

Running towards the love of my life who didn't even know how much she meant to me.

A hand landed on my shoulder and pulled me back,

"Hugh, you can't go in there man. The fire is too big, it's going to collapse". He held me firmly, pulling me back with all his strength.

I grabbed his helmet and hauled his face close to mine, letting him see the tears flooding my eyes and streaming down my cheeks.

"Sophie is inside that building Ace, I need to save her. She needs me and I need her. I have to save her!". Another face infiltrated my mind at that very moment. I saw Lucie in my mind, waiting for me, needing me. I'd come for her, I always would. Nothing would keep me from coming back to that little girl but I could not let Sophie burn in that building. I had to try.

I looked Ace deep in the eyes and my voice wobbled as I told him

"If anything happens to me, you take care of my baby girl Acey. You promise me? You need to promise me!". His eyes were red rimmed, the pain clear in his eyes, this man was like a brother to me.

After what felt like an eternity but was only a few seconds in reality, he gave me a firm nod.

"I promise man, I love that little girl but I need you to make me a promise too!" He was shouting, the adrenaline coursing through both of our bodies. He grabbed the collar of my jacket and hauled me even closer.

I nodded.

"You promise me that you'll come back man. We need you, we all need you .... I love you brother". He pulled me into a hug, I could feel his chest rising and falling rapidly as he desperately tried to compose himself.

"I love you too buddy. I promise". I squeezed the top of his arms firmly before giving him a sharp nod and taking off into the burning building, grabbing a stack of fire retardant blankets on my way inside.

Heat, white hot blinding heat hit me with the force of an hurricane. I could barely see a thing as I stepped inside of the smoke filled café. The fire looked to be coming from the kitchen, it was roaring from the serving hatch and beginning to catch on the tablecloths and chairs.

I couldn't see anyone in the restaurant so began to move closer towards the hallway that led to the bathrooms. The smoke was thick and I was thankful to be wearing the proper equipment, I prayed that Sophie wasn't in here otherwise she would be in a huge amount of pain.

I moved past the kitchen, slowly but methodically. I didn't want to touch a thing in case I triggered something to fall. Something deep within my soul was calling to me, it told me that she wasn't inside the kitchen but she was here. I knew she was, I could feel her.

I moved further down the hallway, it was a little clearer to see down here. There was a fire escape on the far side of the hallway which was open, allowing some of the smoke to escape.

I checked both bathrooms, nothing. No sign of Sophie at all. There was only one door left, I wasn't even sure what it was but something told me to check.

I pulled open the door, it was heavy. It was one of those doors that you could only open from the outside. I knew it just by looking at it. I pulled one of Trudie's massive house plants over towards me and used it to prop open the heavy door before taking a step inside.

The room was filled with smoke, thick soot covering every surface. But I could see something covering the floor, what was that? I bent to take a closer look and used my thick glove to scoop up what I instantly recognised as flour. It was everywhere, as if somebody had been having a food fight in here.

The smoke was beginning to thin since I'd opened the door and I knew deep within my heart that she was in here. I searched every corner, behind every shelf before beginning to pull open the cupboard doors.

The first cupboard was filled with dishes and bowls. The second was filled with sauces and other condiments. And the third was filled with ... my girl. My heart thumped in my chest and tears filled my helmet as I took in the sight before me.

Sophie was curled up in the foetal position in the bottom of a tiny cupboard, a tea towel was held over her mouth and nose, she was covered head to toe in soot and she was completely still.

She didn't react when I pulled open the cupboard door, didn't flinch when I reached in the touch her. As I heaved her into my arms I could see that her chest was moving up and down ever so slightly. If I could have dropped to my knees and prayed to the Gods right there and then I would have done.

I used the bundles of fire retardant blankets to wrap her firmly, covering every single inch of her body before taking off down the hallway towards the fire escape.

I felt the rumble before I heard it, it sounded like thunder and I instantly sensed impending doom. I ran as fast as I could, an unconscious Sophie lying in my arms. Rubble started falling from the ceiling, dust from the plaster adding to the plumes of smoke that surrounded us.

I ran and ran and just as I made it to the fire escape door I heard a boom! The building began to collapse behind me, pieces of debris hitting the ground, narrowly missing us before the doorway collapsed and the building was completely engulfed in flames.

I kept running, I could see blue lights flashing from around the corner of the building. I could hear screaming in the distance, it sounded so far away. Like a pained animal, the howling got louder and louder as I rounded the corner. The road outside Trudie's was crawling with fire engines, ambulances and police trying desperately to cordon off the area.

I ran as fast as I could towards the closest ambulance, the screaming still sounding from somewhere to my right. My first thought was that it was Trudie but it wasn't. As I rounded the side of the ambulance I took in the sight of Ace, on his knees on the concrete, head in his hands as he howled with agony.

I reached up with one hand and yanked the helmet off my head, throwing it to the ground. Nobody had noticed me leaving the building as I'd come from around the back and there was far too much commotion going on.

"Brother!", I shouted.

"Ace!". His head turned around sharply, eyes locking onto mine as he broke down in tears. He sobbed and swiped at his tears before leaping to his feet and running towards me and throwing his arms around my shoulders.

"Thank fuck, I thought, I thought ...".

"It's ok, I'm ok. But Sophie needs help, help me man".

Ace instantly charged forward, me trailing closely behind him.

"Everybody out the way, we need a paramedic!", he shouted loud enough for the village to fall silent. The shouting halted, replaced with shocked gasps and the sound of Trudie's heartbroken sobs, as she rushed towards us with Mitch close on her heels.

I managed to climb into the back of the ambulance and place Sophie on the stretcher. I didn't want her to leave my arms but I knew she had to. She needed help urgently. The paramedics immediately unwrapped her from the blankets and done their thing.

Checking her for injuries, placing an oxygen mask over her beautiful soot covered face.

I couldn't see any burns or other injuries and for that I was thankful, but she still wasn't waking up.

"Why isn't she waking up?" I asked one of the paramedics working on her.

"She's inhaled a lot of smoke Sir, her body is trying to protect itself. We are going to blue light her to the hospital. Are you coming with us?".

I took a seat beside her, held her hand tightly and told him,

"I'm never leaving this woman ever again". The doors slammed shut, Ace giving me a firm nod before they closed.

And for the first time in many years I prayed, I prayed to a God that I didn't necessarily believe in.

*Save her, please save her. Sophie I love you baby, please come back to me.*

# Chapter Thirty-Five

**Sophie**

*"I love you baby", "Please come back to me", "I'm sorry I didn't tell you before but if you just wake up I'll tell you right now".*

I was having the most amazing dream. I could hear Hugh's voice, it sounded so quiet and so far away but it was like a dream come true. He was telling me everything I'd wanted to hear. Why was he so far away?

My eyes were closed and my head was pounding. I felt like my brain was waking up but my body wasn't cooperating. I was laying down, warm and comfortable. I could feel a heat in my hand, a warm palm holding mine tightly, a thumb caressing the back of my hand.

I slowly cracked open my eyes, they felt crusted over like I'd been in a deep sleep for a long time. The blinding sunshine was streaming through the windows to my right, making it difficult for my tired eyes to focus on anything in the room.

After a few seconds I began to piece together what had happened, it hit me like a ton of bricks when I remembered what had happened. The fire, the passing out. *Am I dead?* No I can't be. I slowly looked around the room, I'm in a hospital room. Bright white walls glared back at me, a distant beeping from the machines surrounding me.

As I looked around, I stopped in my tracks when I saw a beautiful head of tousled brown hair. Hugh had his head resting on the side of my bed, holding my hand in his own, he was softly snoring into my side.

I tried to take a deep breath as the emotions ran rampant through my body, I was alive and Hugh was here. He hadn't left me. I had no idea how long I'd been here, all I knew was that my body was stiff, my head hurt and my lungs felt like lead weights inside my chest.

I gently pulled my hand from Hugh's and rested it on top of his head, running my fingers through the soft strands. I was overcome with emotion when I thought about the fact that I may never have gotten to do that ever again.

"Hugh?" I croaked, my voice quiet as I hadn't spoken in a long time.

"Hugh?"

Hugh began to stir, his big shoulders heaving with a yawn as he sat up and rubbed at his red rimmed, swollen eyes. It took him a second to figure out what had woken him, but when he did, his eyes locked onto mine, capturing me in his stare. His eyes darted around my face searching for signs of pain, he still hadn't said a word. I saw the moment the realisation hit him that I was awake, his face crumpled, thick tears streaked down his cheeks and settling in his overgrown beard as he heaved giant sobs into his hands.

"Hughie come here baby,"

Hugh was on his feet and in my arms in an instant, we held each other close as we both cried heavy tears of relief.

"You didn't leave me?" he whimpered.

"Never. I'm here Hughie, I'm here". We held each other for a long time. Hugh crawled onto the bed and snuggled with me under the covers, my head resting on his chest as we both attempted to calm ourselves.

We sat in silence, just soaking each other in before Hugh used his finger on my chin to turn my face to his.

"Honey, I'm sorry. I should have told you this a long time ago, from the moment I felt it.... I love you too baby, with my whole heart. I think I've loved you from the moment we met. I'm sorry I didn't say it back to you that day, I was overcome with guilt and I was truly so terrified to love again. I can't lose you Sophie, you've quickly become my whole world. You're my missing piece, the piece that fills my soul with love and joy. I love you, now and forever. I was so scared that if I let myself love you then I'd open myself up to the agony of losing someone else. But, now I realise that it isn't a choice, I have no choice but to love you, you're written into my very being. I felt like I was betraying Grace but now I know that if I don't live and love then that will be how I let her down. She wanted the world for me and Lucie ... you are the world honey".

Tears were running rivers down my cheeks, collecting on the blanket below me. Could this man seriously be real? I went to respond but he wasn't finished, it was as if he'd been practising his speech while he waited for me to wake up.

"Grace was the first love of my life, Lucie was the second and you my love, are the third and forever love of my life. I want a life with you, I want to get married and have babies. I want to cheer you on when you're doing book signings or making people smile with your cakes. I want to hold you when you cry and get completely lost in you when you smile. I want to live and I want to love you forever". He finished with a sigh, releasing a breath that seemed like it had been stuck inside forever.

I took his head in both hands and pulled him to my lips, kissing him with every ounce of energy I could muster.

"I love you too Hugh and I love Lucie as if she was my own. I want everything you want, forever and always. I thought I had love in my life before but that doesn't even scratch the surface of what I feel you for. You're my person, my best friend, my soul mate. I want to spend the rest of my days wrapped in your arms, watching our little ones learn and grow. I want us to grow old and grey together and be one of those sweet old couples who walk hand in hand with our matching coats and walking sticks. I want forever with you Hughie, starting right now".

"Starting right now," he echoed back.

"First things first though, just to get us started I have a question for you". His eyes were lit up, a smirk pulling at the side of his mouth.

"What's that?" I asked with a small curious smile of my own.

"Will you .......move in with us?". My heart was pounding, the cheeky shit got me all over excited then!

"I would love nothing more than to live with you and Lucie". I paused and that's when I remembered and started to panic. My breathing escalated, the machines started beeping frantically behind me.

"It's ok baby, just breathe, what is it?". Hugh was there, holding me in his arms, pressing kisses to my forehead.

"All my stuff, is it all gone? My books were all inside the apartment, all of my work. Is it gone?". I hung my head, I couldn't lose it all. There's no way I could do all of that again.

"Baby, I've got it. I've got it all, your laptop, your manuscripts, your photos of your parents. They managed to put the fire out before the entire apartment fell into the café. I thought the whole building was collapsing behind me when I pulled you out of there but it wasn't, it was just the plaster and most of the ceiling. Ace went back into your apartment when it was safe and he saved as much as he could. We will need to replace all of your clothes but we got the most important things".

He kept talking but I was still fixating on the part where he said that he pulled me out, I looked into this handsome man's big blue eyes and asked,

"You saved me?".

Hugh held my hand to his mouth, pressing gentle kisses to my knuckles.

"Of course I saved you baby, I'll always save you".

"Oh Hughie, I love you so much. When I was trapped inside a-and I thought I was going to d-die, I prayed for you, I prayed that you'd find me".

"I'll always find you, I'm never letting you go ever again. I hope you don't mind clingy because I'm never letting you out of my sight!" he said with a soft chuckle as the door opened and the doctor strode in.

"Good morning Sophie, how are you feeling?", he asked as he approached me and started checking me over. He gave Hugh a smirk, who was still tucked up in bed with me. He leaned closer and whispered,

"No way am I asking that man to leave your bed, he refused to leave your side in two days". My throat closed up, the overwhelming rush of love I felt for my man was enough to knock me over. I managed to give the doctor a small smile as I held Hugh's hand firmly in mine.

"I'm ok. My throat is really sore, my head is pounding and my lungs hurt. But other than that, I'm ok. Grateful to be here".

"You sustained some pretty bad damage from smoke inhalation. When you first came in we had you on a ventilator to support your airway and give you respiratory support. We've had you on one hundred percent oxygen for forty eight hours to ward off any carbon monoxide poisoning. But all in all you were very lucky Sophie, you just need to take things easy for a couple of weeks. Let your body heal. I would like to see you again in a week just to give you a check over. I'd like to keep you for the rest of the day just so we can keep an eye on things but if you're happy then I'm happy to discharge you. You must come back immediately if you start to feel worse".

I gave him a nod at the same time that Hugh spoke up,

"She's in good hands Doc, I've got her".

He really did have me, in every single sense of the word. He had my heart, he had my soul, he had my body and he had my forever.

# Chapter Thirty-Six

**Sophie**

## *Eight Weeks Later*

I woke to *the* most delicious warmth between my legs. I could feel Hugh's scruff scratching on my inner thighs sending shivers down my spine.

I sat up ever so slightly and pulled up the blanket to see a head of thick brown hair disappearing underneath.

He pressed kisses to my inner thighs whilst running his hands up my legs to pull them apart, I opened for him instantly. He held me open in front of his face, dipping his mouth and devouring me like a starving man at a buffet.

Holy shit, I'd never felt pleasure like it, this man was a magician and I could not get enough of him. He nipped at my lower lips, swirling his tongue around my already swollen clit. It was begging for his attention. He kissed my pussy the same way he'd kiss my lips, the perfect pressure, nipping and sucking. My back arched off the bed as I slipped my hands into his silky hair and held him close whilst I ground against his face.

It didn't take long for the pressure building in my lower stomach to creep up my spine and blow my mind to pieces. I ground on him relentlessly, he never let up, licking me as I shuddered against him. White lights burst behind my eyes, warmth spread through my limbs as I exploded. He kept nipping as I rode out my pleasure.

He scrambled up my body, pressing kisses along the way before taking my mouth with his, I could taste myself on his tongue but I didn't care. I couldn't get enough of this man.

He took his hard length in his hand, squeezing firmly at the base before pointing it towards my entrance and slamming home.

He took me hard and fast, pounding me into the mattress. The grunts and groans coming from his throat turned me on even more and made me insatiable for him. I placed both hands firmly on his arse and pulled him deeper inside me as far as he could go, my pussy stretching around his hardness as he completely bottomed out. It hurt, but it hurt so good. He was a big guy.

Suddenly, he pulled out and flipped me over on to my stomach, placing a pillow under my hips and raising my arse up into the air. I felt like I was totally on display for this man. He must have liked what he saw as I felt his warm mouth attack my pussy with fervour. One long swipe from entrance to clit before firm warm hands grabbed a hold of my hips and his thick cock prodded at my entrance. He bottomed out again in one thrust. He was so hard I could feel every single ridge and groove as he set my body ablaze.

A thick tattooed arm swept across my stomach as he pulled me up onto my knees, my back to his front as he continued to destroy me with his thrusts. He placed both hands on my breasts, kneading them, stroking my nipples into hard peaks.

I couldn't hold back my moans, this man made me feel things I'd never felt before.

Warm lips and a hot tongue licked and nipped at my neck, he pressed soft kisses along my shoulders which was in total contrast to the savage way he was pounding into me. His hands were on the move again, one holding firmly onto my hip. I just knew I'd have small fingerprint bruises littering my skin later on.

The second hand crept up between my breasts and settled on my throat, he held tightly but not enough to constrict my breathing. He squeezed gently.

"Oh baby you like that? You just flooded my cock", he groaned.

"Yes, yes!". I couldn't seem to put a coherent sentence together, Hugh had wiped all the brain cells from my head.

My body began to shake and tremble with the overwhelming pleasure coursing through my body.

"Oh fuck, I'm going to ..." I didn't get to finish my sentence before I exploded again. I went deaf and blind momentarily as my body was taken to heaven. Hugh kept pounding, sucking, kneading, squeezing my throat before he seemed to grow impossibly harder and larger inside of me.

One more hard thrust and he stilled, pulling my hips back tightly into his groin as he spilled his seed deep inside me. We remained that way for long seconds before eventually collapsing into a heap of sweaty limbs.

"Baby?" Hugh muttered breathlessly.

"Hmm?" My brain hadn't yet calmed enough for me to make any sense.

"I know it's soon but ... seeing my come dripping out of you is turning me feral. Wanna make a baby soon? I can't wait to put a baby in you beautiful".

I sat up instantly, jumping into his lap and straddling him again.

"Are you serious?". I couldn't contain the excitement in my voice.

"I'm serious baby, I want forever with you. Why wait?". He had a grin plastered across his face. The change in this man over the past few weeks was incredible. He was free, he loved big and he didn't ever hold back for a second.

"I love you!". I shouted as I slammed my lips to his. Grabbing the base of his cock, which was already hard again, pointing it towards my entrance as I slid all the way down again. Ready for round two.

Later on that day Hugh and I were sat at the dining room table helping Lucie with her arts and crafts, when there was a knock on the front door.

"I'll get it," I giggled, while taking in a glitter covered Hugh. The sight took me back to a very delicious memory that took place at Lucie's birthday party.

I rushed down the hallway and swung open the front door. Trudie and Mitch were stood together underneath a massive umbrella, shielding themselves from the relentless English rain. I hadn't seen them properly for a while, the café was currently closed while it was undergoing reconstruction works after the fire. It turns out that an over worked extension lead had exploded in the kitchen. I was so incredibly lucky that I'd left the room when I had, or the outcome could have been very different.

Trudie instantly pulled me into a warm hug,

"How are you doing sweetie?", she asked. As she stepped back, Mitch grabbed a hold of my shoulders and pulled me close for an awkward hug. He was a very sweet man, quiet, contemplative but he wasn't big on showing affection.

"I'm great thanks, come on in out of the rain. I was just about to put the kettle on". Trudie and Mitch followed me into the dining room, saying their hellos to Hugh and Lucie before taking a seat around the dining table and getting stuck into the arts and crafts.

I went off into the kitchen to prepare teas, coffees and the cherry bake wells Lucie and I had baked this morning before carrying them all in on a large tray and placing them on the table. Everybody helped themselves as I took a seat opposite Trudie.

"So, what do we owe the pleasure of this visit? It's so lovely to see you both". I told them affectionately. They were parental figures to me nowadays, especially Trudie. We were so close I loved her like family.

Whilst the café had been closed I'd really cracked down on my writing. With the support from Hugh and all the encouragement from our friends, I'd self published three of my romance books! They were set to release in the next few weeks and to say I was terrified would be an understatement.

I was doing it for myself and to show Lucie that she should fight for what she wants and believe the voices around her when they tell her she can do something.

"Well sweetie". Trudie placed her tea down on the table and took my hands in hers. For some reason I felt like I should brace myself for bad news, surely we'd had enough bad luck between us to last a lifetime.

"Oh don't fret sweetie, it's nothing bad". Obviously I wasn't very good at hiding my emotions, the worry was written all over my face.

"Ok," I said quietly "What is it?".

"Well ... you're fired". Trudie stated, no preamble, no slowly building up to it. Nope, straight to the point.

"What? Why? You said it wasn't bad news ..." I trailed off in a whisper. Hugh moved to my side and took my hand in his before placing them firmly in my lap.

"What's this about guys? We thought that once the café was complete Sophie would come back and do her usual job for you?", Hugh asked, coming to my defence.

"Well, things have changed I'm afraid dear ... Mitch and I have decided not to reopen the café. We are retiring and going on a month long cruise in the Caribbean!" she said excitedly, bouncing in her seat.

"That's great news, I'm so happy for you both". And I was, but what the hell was I going to do about a job.

"There's more ..." Mitch finally spoke up. "We've decided something ...".

"We are giving you the building honey. For free, as a gift. You were wasted as a waitress, you're such an incredibly talented baker and writer. We want to help you to make all your dreams come true". Trudie said as a silent tear streaked down her cheek.

"But why?" I asked, I was in shock. Hugh squeezed my hand in reassurance.

"Well sweetie, Mitch and I never managed to have children of our own and it was always something we both longed for. It just wasn't in the cards for us, but then you came along. You walked into our café looking like a heartbroken, lost soul and look at you now. You've been through far too much in your life, all totally undeserved. We love you, we are incredibly proud of you and we want this for you. It would mean the world to us if you were to accept".

I was off my feet in an instant and practically throwing myself at the two of them, they both stood silently and wrapped me in their arms. Holding me close, I'd never felt as loved as I did right now, surrounded by so many wonderful people.

"I don't know what to say you guys, it's too much".

Mitch piped up, "You say yes, you make two old people very happy and you take our gift and you make it into something truly wonderful. You put your heart and soul into everything you do and you make us proud, alright?". I think that was the most words I'd ever heard him say, especially all in one go.

"Ok," I said quietly, "Thank you, I promise to make you both proud".

I was incredibly grateful for my life and everybody in it. I was even grateful for all the terrible things I'd been through as they made me even more appreciative of what I had now.

I'd been at rock bottom and it wasn't much fun, but now I was soaring. Soaring towards a bright and happy future and I couldn't wait to get started.

# Chapter Thirty-Seven

**Hugh**

### *Eight Weeks Later*

Today was the day, after being gifted the café eight weeks ago, Sophie had been working flat out to get the bakery bookshop ready. When Trudie and Mitch left her the building, it was restored, completely bare and ready for Sophie to put her stamp on it and make it her own.

The last eight weeks had probably been some of the best of my life. Sophie had moved in and it had been seamless. She fitted right in like she was always supposed to be there. Lucie loved having her around too, it was something she'd never had the chance to experience before. Having a mother figure in the house had been amazing for her and Sophie was just so incredible with her, she would make an amazing mother one day. They had 'girl days' which I was banned from. They went shopping, got their nails done and spent endless hours in the kitchen baking all sorts of delicious goodies. I was allowed to partake in taste testing which of course was the best part, I may have to step up my days at the gym though if I carried on!

We'd spent endless hours together, tending to the vegetable patch or paddling in the stream at the bottom of the garden.

I was beyond happy. I felt at peace and I felt completely free. Receiving that final letter from Grace had allowed me to open up my heart and completely embrace everything Sophie was offering me and my God was she offering a lot. I could not be more in love with that woman if I tried. She was my everything and I cherished every moment with her - especially the naked moments when I got to spend hours between her legs and bury myself deep inside her heart.

Today was the day that the bakery bookshop would open. Sophie insisted on keeping every single detail from me, she wanted it to be a surprise for Lucie and I. I just knew it was going to be a massive hit. She had put her heart and soul into it and spent all of her free time working hard to make it perfect.

Since the fire, Sophie had self published three of her books and had ordered plenty to stock in her very own bookshop, along with all the other mountains of books which were ready to grace the bookshelves. I was so proud of her.

When I met her around six months ago she was a totally broken woman, the sorrow I saw in her eyes had been reflected in my own. Over the months she had been through some shit, some massive hurdles stood in her way but she's overcome ever single one of them, and turned into the strongest woman I've ever known. Her smile lights up every room she walks into, joy follows her and spreads through the hearts of those she loves. She's made a good group of friends and she's finally found the family that she's been searching for.

She's my family, she's Lucie's family. She's the missing piece in our hearts and she's filled it to bursting. I couldn't wait to expand our family and make all of her dreams come true. Sophie had her IUD removed six weeks ago. We knew it was soon, we hadn't even known each other for a year yet. But she was my person and I was hers, we knew that we were forever so why wait. We had both been through enough heartbreak to last a lifetime, we'd both lived through crippling loneliness and pain. There was no reason to hold back any more, we were free. Well almost free, Sophie's divorce from Liam hadn't yet been finalised but in our minds and hearts it was already over.

We both had a past and things that would take a long time to deal with but we were going to move past them together. Sophie would always hold a love for Liam in her heart. She had a huge heart and was somehow able to find forgiveness for him in there. She was a better person that me, if I ever came face to face with that man again then my fist would be meeting his face.

It takes an incredible person to be able to forgive someone who has wronged them in so many ways, but that was one of the main reasons that I'd fallen completely and irrevocably in love with Sophie, she was super human. She was the light in a very dark world sometimes and I hadn't found a single flaw yet. Maybe the snoring, but I actually found that pretty cute.

It was just after midday and Lucie and I had strict instructions to arrive at the new bakery bookshop at precisely twelve thirty for the grand opening. We were so proud of Sophie and so excited to be a part of her new chapter.

We pulled up in the car park opposite, which we struggled to find a parking space in because it was completely jam packed. Crowds lined the streets, patiently waiting to see the new shop. My heart warmed in my chest and thudded hard at the sight of all of these people who had come out to support my girl.

Hand in hand, Lucie and I fought our way to the front as I pulled her little body up into the safety of my arms. Sophie hadn't wanted us to see inside until the big day, I wanted to hold her and comfort her. I knew she was incredibly nervous, but she insisted we wait out front. I was grateful to know that she had the girls inside with her, Lily, Freya and Maisie had spent every free moment they had helping her out. She had fit right in with my crazy bunch of friends and now she had made them her own. We were a great big messy family but we loved each other - apart from Ace and Lily. That relationship was broken, which was a huge shame because they had been best friends since school, long before they had gotten together as a couple.

I hoped for their own sake that they could work past whatever had happened. That in time they could find forgiveness, maybe not as a couple, but as friends. Time would tell, time heals most wounds and if it doesn't completely heal it then it puts a nice plaster on top to dull the ache.

It was finally time for the big reveal, I held Lucie in my arms, surrounded by my boys Ace, Ryan and Mack. My parents were stood next to me, they'd also come out for Sophie's big day. I wasn't surprised, they loved Sophie almost as much as I did!

The doors opened and there was my angel, flanked by her girl-friends as she walked outside and settled between the windows. The building looked beautiful, she had painted it pink in honour of Lucie's favourite colour. There were hanging plants and plant pots adorning the windowsills filled with white daisies, the sight caused my heart to pang with pain in my chest. Grace had always loved daisies and it meant the world to me that Sophie always remembered. Whenever I visited Grace's grave there was always a fresh bunch of daisies there for her and I just knew in my heart that they were from Sophie. She never mentioned visiting, but I knew she did. Just another reason to love her.

My thoughts were silenced when Sophie began to speak, I could hear the tremble in her voice as she fought against her nerves,

"Hello everybody and thank you so much for all coming out for my special day. I can't tell you how humbled and grateful I am that you could all be here.

Before I let you all inside I just wanted to take a moment to thank a few people. Firstly, none of this would be possible without Trudie and Mitch. I cannot thank you enough for this gift, I hope to make you proud and I promise that I will take good care of it. Secondly, my friends ... you have been so incredibly supportive of me since the moment you laid eyes on me. You are my family and I love you all so much.

My next thank you is to little Lucie Lu. I love you sweet pea, you've opened up my heart and filled it with joy. You are the sweetest little girl in the whole world and I am so thankful that I get to be a part of your life everyday and watch you grow.

My Hughie," her voice cracked as her eyes met mine, Freya put her arm around her shoulders and pulled her close, kissing her temple and whispering words of encouragement. My own throat closed up and tears burned behind my eyes.

"My Hughie," she continued "I've never felt a love like ours, so strong and unconditional it's overwhelming. I waited my whole life for you, we've been through so much but I truly believe that we found each other when we were meant to. I love you big baby and I always will. Thank you for finding me, thank you for saving me and thank you for loving me," tears fell silently down her cheeks, mirroring mine as Lucie pulled me close and kissed them away.

"There's just one more person that I have to thank. Unfortunately she can't be here with us today but I know she's looking down on us all and giving us all the love and strength we need.

Grace Weston was an incredible woman, an amazing wife and a beautiful mother. I may not have gotten the pleasure to meet her but I know deep in here" she held both hands to her heart "we would have been good friends. She had a big heart, that's reflected in her husband and her daughter. She deserved the world but sadly that was taken from her. Instead, she gave it to me. She gave me her world and I'll forever hold it close to my heart. I hope I can make her proud and shower her family with the love they deserve, I have an incredible woman to live up to". Sophie's red rimmed eyes looked up to the sky, as one we all looked up with her. "We love you Grace, we miss you and you will never be forgotten. Which brings me to my final point which is ..." Her voice cracked again as she struggled to regain her calm.

"This is for you Grace, it's for us to remember you and it's a place for you to live on in our hearts". Sophie walked over to the window and grabbed a hold of a long rope attached to the covering hiding the name of the bakery bookshop from view.

"Without further a do, I'd like to welcome you to .... Letters To Grace". Sophie pulled the rope and there it was, I was completely stunned silent. The words Letters To Grace were made entirely from daisies. She'd named her shop after my late wife. Seriously how did I manage to deserve this woman. I strode forward with three large steps and pulled Sophie into my arms, I didn't have any words. Nothing would do my feelings justice. We held each other, Lucie sandwiched in the middle, as happy tears fell down our cheeks and roaring applause sounded behind us.

Everybody was crying, there wasn't a dry eye in the street, even the guys were in floods of tears.

We cut the ribbon together, the three of us as a family, as we welcomed everybody inside the most beautiful shop I'd ever seen in my life. To the right was the bookshop, bookshelves filling the walls top to bottom. Comfy sofas and armchairs dotted around the room along with tables to sit at. In one corner of the room was a huge tree, inside the damn room, how incredible is that. The front had been cut open and inside were book shelves filled with children's books, little glass characters hanging from the branches and fluffy pillows filling the bottom. It had Mack written all over it, him and his chainsaw!

There was a pink heart shaped table right in the middle with all of my girls books arranged beautifully on top, along with small vases filled with fresh daisies dotted in between.

There were so many little details my eyes couldn't take them all in. Picture frames on the walls holding famous quotes, colourful butterflies dotting the walls, flower canopies hanging from the ceiling. It was unbelievable. There had been no expense spared thanks to Liam finally doing the right thing and setting Sophie up for life. She put her heart and soul into this place.

To the left was the bakery and when I tell you this place smells incredible, I can't even explain it. Round white tables with pretty pink tablecloths, more vases filled with daisies. The shop was stunning. But it was when I looked behind the counter, right in the centre of the shop that my heart stuttered in my chest. Right there was a photo of my Grace, on a canvas. It was my favourite photo of her, she was dancing through a meadow of daisies, her thick brown hair flying behind her in the wind as she smiled brightly at the camera. Next to the photo were the words 'Gone but never forgotten'.

This place was for Grace and I'd always love her, she would always be in my heart. But right now it was time to move on, she had set me free and I prayed that she was at peace.

I'd had lots of dreams in my life and so far every single one of them had come true, some had been broken but others held firm.

It wasn't until later on that night when we were tucked up in bed, held close in each others arms after hours of love making, that Sophie made another one of my dreams come true when she whispered the words "We made a baby Hughie".

I looked at my woman, the love of my life and holder of my heart and fell even more in love with her.

If life has taught me anything it's to hold on to the good moments, treasure them in your heart forever and keep them close. We have to go through the hard times to teach us how to appreciate the good. Grief will always be there, but it's a badge of honour. It means that we loved someone enough that they left little scars on our hearts. We will always miss them, but it's ok to set them free and find love and light in our lives again.

# Epilogue

## Sophie

It was early December and I was thirty one weeks pregnant with our little boy, who was currently kicking the hell out of my bladder as I walked around the Christmas tree farm with my family.

We were all here, Mack and Maisie who was also pregnant with their first child, a little girl. Freya and Ryan who were newly married. Ace and Elodie, now that was a rocky beginning for them! Blimey it was like something out of a dark romance novel but it all worked out in the end. Lily was there too, her and Ace still weren't on the best of terms but they were now able to be around each other without us all feeling on edge.

Then there was Hugh and Lucie, my people. Not long after the opening of Letters To Grace, Lucie had asked if she could start calling me Mama. We all burst into tears when she uttered the words that had meant more to me than anything.

*"Sophie, you know you have a baby in your tummy and that they are going to get to call you Mama?".*

*"Yes?" I'd replied, not entirely sure where this line of questioning was heading.*

*"Well ... I know that my first Mummy is in heaven. But ... c-can you be my Mama too?".*

*"Oh baby, I would love to be your Mama more than anything else in the whole wide world. I love you princess".*

*"I love you too Mama". She whispered as I held her close.*

That was a day I'd never forget, the day I became a mother. The day my dream came true.

We were walking slowly through the Christmas tree farm trying to find the perfect tree when deja-vu hit me. This time last year, Hugh held me up against a wall and ground us both to orgasm before spilling all over the grass. I felt my cheeks heat as I looked over at the man beside me who was seemingly remembering the same moment that I was. I was way too pregnant to recreate that moment now but one day we would.

As we rounded the corner to where that fateful day had happened, I stopped dead in my tracks with shock. It was stunning, the surrounding trees were covered in twinkling fairy lights, the snow covered ground was scattered with red rose petals, soft music started playing from ... somewhere. I couldn't figure out where but I recognised it immediately, it was 'Love The Hell Out Of You' by Lewis Capaldi, my favourite song.

I looked around at the smiling faces of our friends, what the hell was going on. I wasn't kept waiting long before it was pretty damn obvious what was going on. My man was on the ground in front of me, on one knee, holding the most exquisite diamond ring I'd ever seen. Beside him was our daughter, also down on one knee, holding a matching diamond bracelet with the word 'Mama' clearly visible.

My hands flew to my mouth, tears already trickling down my cheeks as I took in the sight before me. Everybody else faded away when Hugh began to speak, his deep voice wobbling, every word cracking as he struggled through his speech.

"Sophie, you came into our lives when we needed you the most. You completely filled the missing piece in our hearts and made us whole again.

We treasure you every single day and thank the heavens for sending you our way. You made my heart beat again and it beats only for you baby, forever and always.

I can't imagine a life without you, you're my world, my heart, my soul. You are my forever and my happy ever after. Will you do me the great honour of becoming my wife? Honey, will you marry me?".

"Will you marry me too Mama?", the sweetest little voice followed Hugh's. How could I ever refuse? These two people and the little one on the way were the absolute loves of my life.

"Yes! Yes! Yes! Forever yes!" I shouted and threw myself into their arms.

Cheers sounded around us, our friends so incredibly happy for us as Hugh pulled both Lucie and I into his strong arms, holding us closely as we slow danced in the middle of the Christmas tree farm. Our friends surrounding us, snowflakes falling from the sky and our hearts full and happy.

Eight weeks later, we welcomed our son into the world. Little Beau Ace Weston was born surrounded with love. Every single one of my dreams had come true and I couldn't wait to enjoy them for the rest of my life.

For someone who just over a year ago had been so incredibly lost, I felt truly thankful that I'd finally been found.

## The End

# Extended Epilogue

*Want a little more of Hugh and Sophie?*
*Check out their extended epilogue here:*
*https://csmithbooks.onlineweb.shop/page/bonus-content*

*Also, it would mean the world to me if you could leave me a little review on Amazon – thank you!*

*Want to learn more about Jax our friendly pub landlord? Sign up to my newsletter to receive his novella for free.*
*Hint: He wasn't always a wholesome pub landlord!*
*https://csmithbooks.onlineweb.shop/*

*What's Next...*

*Are you ready for Mack and Maisie's novella? One chance encounter and a hot and steamy night leads to a lifetime of highs, lows and a whole load of happiness.*
*Found and Flirty is coming soon!*
*Follow along on Instagram for updates on this release.*
*Find me at c.smith_ books*

## Finding Forever Series

Lost And Found is Book One in the Finding Forever series, there are four more books to go!

The series will be as follows:

Book One: Lost And Found – Hugh And Sophie's Novel.

Book Two: Found And Flirty – Mack And Maisie's Novella.

Book Three: Lost And Forever – Ace And Elodie's Novel.

Book Four: Found And Free – Ryan And Freya's Novella.

Book Five: Lost And Forgiven – Kit And Lily's Novel.

# Acknowledgements

My lovely husband Rich, for always going along with my hectic ideas and supporting me every step of the way. By working hard and providing for us all you have given me the opportunity to follow my dreams, for that I am forever grateful.

My beautiful children, you've taught me what true love really is. You are my inspiration. You are my entire world and I only hope that you grow up to be kind, hard working people who follow your dreams.

Mum, you have supported me from day one. You've always hyped me up in whatever I've wanted to do. I can't thank you enough for everything you've done for me in my life. You mean the world to me.

Dad, thanks for the steady flow of takeaways to take the pressure off! And for always supporting me in everything I've chosen to do. I love you.

Siblings, I couldn't have asked for a better brother and sister to grow up with. Even though you're both annoying! (Love you really!)

Roy, you've always treated me like I was your own flesh and blood. You're the best father in law a girl could ask for.

Natalie, for being my very best friend, for always listening to me moan and complain. You're my sounding board and I'm forever grateful that I found you.

Kerry, you have helped me every single step of the way with this book, thank you. Thank you for book club too, I always look forward to our laughs!

And lastly, my Nanny Prim. This book is for you, even though the thought of you reading all of those sex scenes made me cringe! You give the best hugs, I love you with all my heart. I hope I've made you proud.

# About The Author

C.Smith was born and raised in Hastings in the South Of England, she now resides a little further along the coast in Hampshire. When she's not writing, she can usually be found with a nose in someone else's book.

C.Smith is happily married with two young children. She loves anything creative, whether it be writing, crochet or playing around with vinyl.

She is currently working full time as a romance author and creating fun merchandise for her online store https://csmithbooks.onlineweb.shop/

For more updates, visit her website linked above, sign up to her newsletter to receive her free novella or find her on Instagram at c.smith_books

Printed in Great Britain
by Amazon

40509039R00138